When I got to Lucy's door, I paused to see if I could hear anything coming from her room. Nothing. I knocked and opened it. Again, the smell hit me. It was stronger this time. I had to suppress the urge to gag. I reached over and felt along the wall. As soon as my palm landed on the switch, I flipped it. Lucy laid there in her bed, but her eyes were not closed.

PRAISE FOR THE
WORKS OF DANIELLE DEVOR

Named Examiner's 2014 Women in Horror:
93 Horror Authors You Need to Read Right Now

"SORROW'S POINT was probably one of the most terrifying books I've ever read. The book is a page-turner, but definitely not for the faint of heart. There were a few chilling scenes that will leave me with nightmares for weeks."

- Heather Wood, Book Chatter

"DeVor weaves a clever plot and brings the reader a huge mixture of emotions such as fear, anxiety, wonderment and complete shock."

- Romance Thriller Author, Lilian Roberts

'SORROW'S POINT is a great horror story read. For me, this harkens back to the books of my youth, where the mystery and the horror were the main characters."

- Paranormal Mystery Author, Rebecca Trogner

"Move over, Stephen King. Danielle DeVor is on her way!"

- YA Paranormal Romance Author, Katie O'Sullivan

"SORROW'S POINT by Danielle DeVor is a new take on *The Exorcist* and for me a much better read. The author has invoked pure spine-tingling flesh-crawling terror from every chilling page."

- Fantasy and Horror Author, Simon Okill

BOOK ONE OF THE MARKER CHRONICLES

SORROW'S POINT

DANIELLE DEVOR

CITY OWL
PRESS

SORROW'S POINT
The Marker Chronicles: Book One

CITY OWL PRESS
www.cityowlpress.com

Cover Design by Tina Moss. All stock photos licensed appropriately.

For information on subsidiary rights, please contact the publisher at info@cityowlpress.com.

Print Edition ISBN: 978-0-9862516-4-1
Digital Edition ISBN: 978-1-5199976-6-1

Printed in the United States of America

For my father, the real-life Jimmy Holiday.

Good thing you never had to battle a demon,

they wouldn't stand a chance.

- Danielle

Chapter One

The Devil's Brood

1950

WHAT WAS LEFT of O'Dell's hair blew in the wind like the last strands of cotton candy left in the machine. But it was too damn hot to have the windows up. With the sun beating down and the extra weight he'd put on over the last few years, the drive up the hill to Blackmoor turned hotter than an inferno. This year it'd been a hard summer. He'd lost count of the amount of times he had to yell at kids for messing with the fire hydrants.

He adjusted his uniform, pulling at the hem of his shirt. The stiff fabric clung to his skin like nothing else. In this heat, he'd rather be home in his cotton undershirt, sitting on the back porch and drinking a beer. But work came first.

O'Dell parked the cruiser in the drive and looked up at the monstrosity before him. Damn thing was massive—about double the size of a football field. Three levels to it. Way too huge for any normal family, but then, the Blacks were anything but normal. To him, the house seemed like *Moby Dick*: massive, vengeful and misunderstood. He grabbed his hanky and wiped the sweat off the back of his neck.

"Just what I need, Black breathing down my neck. To hell

with you, Doris."

He closed the car door as he stretched the kinks out of his neck and took in his surroundings. No birds or any little creatures stirred. No sound could be heard other than the ragged snorts of his own breath. Goosebumps traveled up his arms. He walked the stone steps to the front door and pressed the button. The doorbell peeled in some tinkling tune O'Dell couldn't name.

He waited.

No one came to the door.

Failing at the entrance, he wandered around. The place was so big it took a while to find the back. By the time he got there, his breath tore out of him and the air felt like twenty pounds in his lungs.

"Goddamn humidity."

He stood in some sort of garden area. Flowers bloomed in beds arranged strategically about the back of the house, like something you'd see in an art book. A stone patio graced the top of the steps. He hobbled up them, still panting. The porch was large enough to host a "quiet" party of three hundred people. Yes, the Blacks were a whole different breed.

He knocked on the back door. Still no answer.

Then, he heard it, a noise at last, a thump from inside the kitchen. He peered in the side window.

It was too much for his brain to process. Flashes blinked in rapid succession as if his mind could only handle it in pieces. Red ran over the walls like a sprayed Jackson Pollock painting. It covered the doorway and dripped from the top as bright as cherry syrup. On the kitchen sink rested a dish drainer. Long black hair pooled around the severed head of Mrs. Black. The blood dripping from the neck stump had matted the hair to the counter.

O'Dell turned away from the windows and puked. Nothing

like this ever happened in Sorrow's Point. The most he usually dealt with was a stupid kid shoplifting from the five and dime. He flew off the patio to the front of the house in record time. His sides ached and his head swam. Nausea beat at his gut. Fumbling with the driver's side door of his cruiser, he jerked it open, hopped inside, and pulled out his radio.

"Jesus Fucking Christ!" He wiped his mouth with the back of his hand and pressed the button on the receiver. "Mable?"

"What?" Mable answered, the receiver crackling.

"I need goddamn backup at Blackmoor!"

"What? Oh God. Sorry, Walt. I'll make the call."

O'Dell released his radio and waited. The sour-sweet smell of the vomit on his shoes turned his stomach. He forced the bile back down his throat.

One at a time, the deputies arrived. For a town the size of Sorrow's Point, two deputies was all the town could afford. O'Dell's fist tightened on the handle as he got out of his car.

"Sheriff, what's going on?" Deputy Jones asked.

Boy was a young one, fresh out of the academy. O'Dell hoped he'd be able to pull his weight. He took a deep breath. "It's bad, Jake. Real bad."

Jones glanced over at the other deputy, Parker, and then turned back to the sheriff. "I've never seen you this messed up, Sheriff. You okay?"

The sweat dripped from O'Dell's head in rivulets. He glanced at his reflection in the side mirror of his cruiser. His face flushed bright red. Before this case was done, he'd need more blood pressure pills. He threw his hat into the dirt. "No, I'm not fucking okay. Black has gone and killed his whole family!" He poked Jones in the chest. "I want you to go get that sumbitch. Cuff his ass and get him in the car. You hear me?"

Jones swallowed. O'Dell watched his Adam's apple bob. Then the deputy motioned for his partner.

"Go round back," O'Dell said.

#

Jones crept around the side of the massive home. He looked this way and that like they had taught him in the academy. This was the first time something serious had gone down in Sorrow's Point. He set his jaw, bound and determined to do the best damn job he could.

The sheriff's footprints pressed into the tall grass, making it easy for him to know where to look. They led him to the back of the house and stopped as soon as they reached the stone patio. Something smelled sour-sweet. Flies would be swarming along soon. He walked up the steps and across to the door. The aroma grew stronger, but he didn't notice anything else out of the ordinary. Suddenly, his foot slid and he almost fell. His eyes drifted to the patio. A pile of puke, almost the same color as the stone, coated the bottom of his boot. "Great."

Backing up a step, he wiped the sole on the stone as best he could. Then, he sidestepped the puddle and peered in the window. Black sat at a butcher block table, facing the window. His dark hair stood up from his head in all directions. Eyebrows arched like the Devil's own. The deep red blood covered him from head to toe. He took another bite out of the small human leg he held in his large hands, grinding his teeth through the raw flesh.

"Oh shit." Jones shook, unable to release his death grip on the windowsill. The world shifted.

Jones peered down the smoking barrel of his gun, following the path through the broken window. He hadn't meant for the gun to go off. He didn't even remember reaching for his weapon. Black's chin slumped against his chest, the back of his head gone. Bits of gray matter stuck to the wall behind him. Black's fingers relaxed. The leg fell to the floor.

Chapter Two

Things to Start With

Present

HERE I WAS, sleeping in my bed, warm and relaxed, when the phone rang. To a lot of people, a phone call is a mundane thing, an everyday occurrence that, for the most part, has no bearing on daily life. But this phone call, it was something else entirely.

I glanced at the clock—3:00 a.m., the true witching hour. I grimaced. That was the last thing I needed to be thinking about. I blinked the sleep from my eyes and groaned. The phone rang again. *Are you kidding me?* I reached for it.

"Jimmy?" the voice asked.

I wiped my hand over my face to try to wake up. *Who in the hell is this?* I threw the covers off my legs and rose. Then, turned and dangled them over the side of the bed. It hit me. I recognized this voice. Someone from my past, someone I hadn't heard from in years. The voice, after all this time, seemed somehow unchanged. "Will?"

His breath hissed into the phone. "I'm sorry for calling so late."

Why was he apologizing? I wasn't sure. The deed had already been done. I'd be lucky to get back to sleep at all.

He coughed. "It's about Lucy."

A buzzing started in my brain and drifted over my body like a swarm of locusts. I had better shit to do with my time—like sleep. He was calling, waking me up, for someone I didn't even know? "Lucy who?"

"Lucy," his pause weighted the air, "my daughter."

Someone sucked all the oxygen out of my lungs with a shop-vac. I bent at the waist, doubled over. A long time ago, Will and I had been great friends. I hadn't spoken to him in who knew how long. It had been before I'd entered seminary for sure. Still though, I didn't even know he was married, but then, maybe he wasn't. Stuff wasn't all that cut and dry these days. "I," starting awkwardly, I took a breath to center and tried again, "I didn't know you had a daughter, Will."

"Aw, hell." A thud reverberated over the line. "Shit. Has it been that long?"

I rolled my eyes. *Yes, you idiot, it's been years.* "Yes, it's been that long."

"Well damn, but ah," he said and honked his nose as he blew it into the phone. "I have a question."

One or many, I wondered, but said simply, "Okay."

"My daughter needs help, and I don't know what to do."

Not a question. I wiped my eyes with the back of my hand, trying to rub the sleep out of them. "What's going on, Will?"

He took a deep breath then hit me with the two ton question he had failed to speak earlier. "Do you still believe?"

My brows wrinkled together. A common habit. My mother used to comment on it all the time. It irritated the hell out of me. But this shit with Will wasn't making any sense. "What are you talking about?"

"God. I'm talking about God."

Oh Christ. I hadn't been asked that question for a long time. Ten years at least. And, then, it hadn't been a very happy occasion. "Yes, I still believe."

Another shaking breath told me this wasn't going to go well. "Can I meet you somewhere?"

I sat up straighter. Somehow, I had a feeling this could easily turn into one of those stories I would tell at the local bar so people could laugh over drinks. "Now?"

"Please, Jimmy. I know this is a lot to ask, but I'm desperate."

I rolled my head to stare at the ceiling. My breath escaped out of my lungs in a hiss. My shoulders slumped. Any chance at sleep disappeared. I was going to kick myself, but I couldn't avoid the inevitable. "Where are you?"

"Sitting in your driveway."

I snatched the phone away from my mouth. "Are you shitting me?" I jumped up and pulled back the curtain next to the bed. Sure enough, a green Toyota 4Runner that had seen better days sat idle in the driveway. I waved, let the curtain fall, and hung up the phone.

Damn creepy. My insides churned like I'd walked off a roller coaster. Something was wrong about this whole situation. Someone I hadn't talked to in over fifteen years randomly showing up at my house in the middle of the night?

I dropped the phone on my bed. "Hell." Bed looked good right now, going downstairs didn't. I left my room, stumbling. When I hit the bottom step, I turned on the hallway light. It bathed the room in a harsh yellow glow that stung my eyes. As I opened the front door, he stood there, blonde hair mussed, face white, hands shaking. What had happened to him?

"Come in," I said.

He stepped over the threshold and the wooden floor popped. We both jumped.

"Don't worry about it. It's an old house." It still left me uneasy. That floor had never popped there before. The overactive imagination I had wanted to cue in the creepy music.

He hobbled in and headed straight to my living room. Narrowly avoiding my pile of books, he plopped in my old brown recliner. I shuffled my feet on the brown shag carpet, dreading this conversation. I sat opposite him on the sofa.

"I'm scared, Jimmy." He blurted it out with nothing to back it up.

I shook my head. "I'm not trying to be cruel here, but what's that got to do with me?"

He leaned forward in the chair and looked me in the eyes. "I need a priest."

"Okay." I sighed. I should have known. This was going to be so much fun. "But I'm not a priest, Will."

He stared at me. "Why not?"

Oh, God. Where in the hell did I start? "Look, it's not that easy of a story."

"I'd like to know," Will said.

Fine. Not like it was a secret, so what the hell. I was too tired to refuse and it all started tumbling out of my mouth like teeth that had been busted out by a prizefighter. "My mother always said we were related to Doc Holliday, so maybe, somehow, I was trying to live up to the importance or something. But since our names weren't even spelled the same, I kind of doubted it."

Will waved a hand at me to continue.

I sighed, liking this less and less. Looking into my old friend's eyes snapped something inside me. It felt wrong and irritating and my blood pressure rose. The whole sordid affair came pouring out of me. I wondered idly how long I had kept it down. "My folks were both alcoholics. I don't know if you knew that, but it's true. Dad was a nice drunk. Mom always had these grandiose ideas." I scratched my arm and stared at the floor.

"I remember her. She kind of always had her nose in the

air," Will said.

"Then you know exactly what I'm talking about," I replied. "Anyway, growing up wasn't exactly cushy. I probably don't react the same way as regular people. In a roundabout way, that's how I ended up becoming a priest. Church was the one place I felt relaxed. My mom was always bickering at my dad about this or that. Sometimes, I wonder if she drove him to drink, but I know better. There was a darker story beneath all of that."

Suddenly, a loud crash interrupted my sad tale as the noise echoed against the side of the house.

"What the fuck was that?"

Will and I jumped. I ran out the front door and around the yard. My garbage cans were knocked over. I could just barely make out a striped tail as the animal ran away.

"Dammit."

I was breathing hard, like I'd just run a marathon. Too much stress and not enough sleep. I glanced at Will.

"Well, that was interesting," he said.

My look turned to glares. It wasn't interesting. It was a pain in my ass. "You aren't funny."

His face paled. "I wasn't meaning to be."

I ignored him and went back inside. I just wanted this over and done with and him out of my house. But it was ironic that my house had been normal and fine before he'd arrived. Now, odd little shit kept happening—the popping floor, the trashcans crashing—and I was getting close to ripping my hair out.

When Will came back into the house, he seemed almost energized. Excited, maybe. He sat in the recliner. "Okay. I want to finish hearing this."

I had been hoping he forgot, but whatever. If telling him got him gone, so be it. "When I was fourteen, Father O'Malley asked if I'd thought about becoming a priest. All it took was that question and I figured it was the thing to do. As soon as I graduated from high school, I entered the seminary and that was that."

"And I went off to college."

I hummed my ascent. "It's been a long time."

He paused as if formulating words. "So I get the start, but why aren't you a priest anymore?"

It wasn't any of his damn business, and frankly, he was a bit too nosy. But if I didn't get it all out, I'd have to talk about it sometime to someone. He was as good as any. "I was fine until I finished seminary and continued 'going out amongst the people.' That's when I met Tabby. She didn't go to the church I was assigned. She didn't go to church at all. I would see her, long red hair blowing in the wind, walking past my church every day. Finally, one day I spoke to her. From that first word, I was done for. The church no longer held me. It was the beginning of the end."

I remembered it all like it was only a few minutes ago. Hell, I even remembered the smell of her. "I fell for her fast. Ironically, we didn't even have a physical relationship at that point. But a parishioner noticed I was spending a lot of time with a pretty young lady. I guess she figured that since Tabby was pretty and I was young, she needed to say something." I clenched my fists together then released them. Thinking about it still made me want to punch something. "I hadn't turned my back on my vows then, but the parishioner used poetic license and contacted my superiors. I was pissed—not only at the little old biddy who lied, but at my superiors for believing her instead of me. They wanted me to change dioceses and get away from Tabby as fast as possible. I had had enough. When I refused to stop seeing Tabby and wouldn't move, they defrocked me."

"Jesus," Will said. "And here I thought something like a church would be above shit like that."

I stretched my fingers, aching to clench them again. "It's that free will thing. Some people are assholes. At any rate, I had a hell of a debt to pay off. When you leave the church—whether you're kicked out or you quit, you have to pay the church back for your education. Tabby and I tried to stick together, but it wasn't working. Eventually, we parted ways. I got a degree in Graphic Design, began working professionally, and minus my irritation about the past, I've been pretty happy ever since." I ran a hand through my hair. "My life in a nutshell."

"It doesn't change things, Jimmy," he said, his eyes capturing mine, searching. "I still need a priest."

My heart started pounding in my chest for no good reason. I'd never had a panic attack as far as I knew, and none of this was cause for one. I focused back on Will. "And I can't help you."

A haunted, sunken look circled his pupils. What caused it, I had no idea, but it was unsettling to see him that unhinged. "I know," he said. "But *they* won't listen to me, and Lucy needs one."

This was beyond catch up with Jimmy. "Why do you think Lucy needs a priest?"

Will wiggled out of his coat and laid it on the floor beside the recliner. His arms were scratched so badly, like he'd recently tangled with a lion.

"See what she did to me?" His eyes grew wider than I thought possible. I was afraid they were going to fall out of his head. "She's possessed."

I sat back. This was way beyond me. You don't randomly hear someone talk about possession every day. Nor see injuries to rival an ill-fated hunter's. "Why do you say that?"

His face turned serious, lines forming across his forehead. "Because she is."

Only I would get someone off their rocker looking for an exorcist at three-o-clock in the morning. For the person to be someone I knew, an old friend, made it all the more strange. The weirdness was stacking up. "Are you sure? Have you thought about taking her to a psychiatrist?"

His hands clenched the armrests of the chair hard enough that his knuckles turned white. With his face growing redder than an apple, his eyes seemed to bulge from their sockets. "She was in a fucking hospital for two weeks!" He jumped out of the chair and began pacing across my floor. "They did nothing for her, and they wouldn't after she almost gouged out a nurse's eye."

Normal took a nose dive off a cliff and I was in a basket. "How old is Lucy?"

He stopped midstride. "Six."

I peered at him, trying to discern the truth in his words. "You're telling me a six-year-old almost gouged out a nurse's eye?"

"Yes." He dropped into the recliner again.

"Will, that could be a bunch of things—"

"We haven't talked about the cat."

The more I heard, the more I wondered if it was Will who needed the psychiatrist.

He stared at me, but more so, he stared through me, lost in his thoughts. I didn't know what to do. Even when I was a priest, I never had anything like this happen. And then you add in the vibe he'd brought with him...a sick, twisted energy. Like poltergeist shadowing the room.

It was going to be a long night.

I rose from the couch and headed to the kitchen. It was too damn late, and I needed some caffeine. My kitchen was a galley style that hadn't been updated since the seventies, but I liked it. Green refrigerators rocked, no matter what anyone else tried to tell me. And the energy didn't follow me there.

I pulled out the coffee maker and got it started. Then I went back into the living room. Will hadn't changed positions.

He whipped his head around, fast and sharp. "Can we turn on some more lights?"

I glanced around. The hallway light provided enough for me to see fine. I couldn't read in it, but it wasn't uncomfortably dark—at least not to me. Maybe the darkness he felt was creeping up on him. Maybe it was something more. I switched on the lamp.

"I can't stand the dark." He scrubbed a hand over his face. "I know you think I'm crazy."

Yeah, he seemed crazy all right, but I wasn't about to tell him that. "You seem scared."

He nodded. "I feel safe here."

I shrugged. I had no idea if I could do anything to help him. And some of the stuff he was saying, and feeling, he'd brought with him. How worse off was he at home? "Will, I need to know what's going on. The whole story."

"I know." He took a deep breath. "I wish I'd never gone to Sorrow's Point."

Chapter Three

Sorrow's Point

WILL WRUNG HIS hands over and over before speaking again. The additional light seemed to help, but his brows continued to furrow as if he struggled to find the words. This was not the Will I'd known. The one I'd known had been kind of a bad ass. After a time, he spoke, "Before I saw the house, I saw the town."

There was a pause, almost like a heartbeat. A single one you hear right before someone takes their last breath. Chills ran up my arms.

I opted for a distraction, a typical sarcastic moment to lighten the mood. "You have to admit, Sorrow's Point is a great name for a town."

"Oh, it gets better than the name." He smiled briefly, but it didn't reach his eyes. Last I remembered, he had bright pale blue eyes. They were much darker now.

"Sorrow's Point is like any other small town," he said. "Everyone knows everybody else's business, the police chief has doubled as the town librarian on more than one occasion, and nothing ever happens there—at least that's what they tell you."

He stared into his palms. His nails were scraggly; he'd clearly been biting them. I didn't know if he was expecting to see blood like Lady Macbeth, but he focused on his hands a little too much.

"It has no Starbucks," he continued on. "No Wal-Mart, and only one fast food restaurant. There's a small elementary school, and the middle school and high school exist comfortably in the same building. Looking at the town, you feel transported back in time." He paused, glancing from his hands and turned to me. "Is the coffee done yet?"

"Dunno, I'll check." Grabbing a couple of mugs from the dish rack, I checked the coffeemaker. When it finished making gurgling sounds, I poured Will and myself a cup. "You take anything in it?" I asked him, sticking my head out of the kitchen so he could hear me.

"Black is fine," he said.

His jumpiness had me nervous. The energy was floating through the air, almost crackling. I could feel it on my skin, a festering malignancy

I stepped back into the kitchen. And then, a coldness struck me. The window over the sink lay wide open, the curtains blowing in the cool breeze. I froze. There was no memory of opening it, and if it had been open very long, I would have felt the cold before now. I shivered. I had enough to worry about. But if this type of crap kept happening after Will left, I was going to need an exorcist.

I clutched the mugs and made my way back into the living room. Maybe caffeine would help us both. Shit, at this point, I was willing to try almost anything. I didn't dare tell Will about the kitchen. He was already unhinged enough as it was. And that was the reason I didn't mention what had happened with the damn window. No need to add to his delusions or whatever they were.

Will had finally gotten comfortable, having taken his shoes off and placing them next to his coat on the floor. I handed him a mug and sat back on the couch.

He took a sip of his coffee and set the mug on the table next to the recliner. "Where was I?"

"The town," I said. I found myself looking off into the shadows left by the places the light didn't reach. Almost as if I was waiting for monsters to come out of the closet.

He nodded. "Sorrow's Point is located among the Blue Ridge Mountains of Virginia. At one time, coal was big business, but now, its main income comes from the hikers passing through the Appalachian Trail." He took another sip, the mug shaking in his hands. "When I first saw it, I thought it was the perfect little town. But like all small towns, there are secrets, hidden away like Aunt Marge's Christmas present. I never really thought about how dangerous secrets can be, but as I found out, in Sorrow's Point, the secrets can kill you."

"Jesus, Will. Do you have any idea how crazy you sound?" I scrunched my brows. He seemed to be trying to distance himself from anything that caused him pain. He focused on the town's history, the smallness and quaintness, the secrets, anything but his problem. From the clear exhaustion and hurt radiating from him like a halo, I wasn't sure it was working very well. Already I'd gotten in way over my head.

He grinned at me. "You don't sound like a priest."

I couldn't help laughing. I'd heard that before. "How is a priest supposed to sound? Granted, I probably shouldn't have taken the Lord's name in vain, but that's a minor sin. Plus, it says nowhere in the Bible that you can't cuss. The church created those rules over time. Not God."

"That's why I came to see you. You're the only one I know crazy enough to believe me."

"And why is that?"

"Well," he tapped his chin idly, "because you had all that stuff happen."

I blinked. I hadn't thought about *that stuff* in a while, but I knew right away what he meant. "You mean my sister's death?"

He had the sense to look chagrined. "Yes."

I didn't like being reminded of it. And it showed just how clueless the man really was. Candy's death was not something I talked about, back then or now. But I rationalized that he was here not for himself, but for his kid. He wasn't thinking straight. I needed to keep that in mind. "And your daughter?"

"Lucy." He dug into his pants pocket, pulling out his wallet. Then he flipped through it and held it out to me.

I took it reluctantly. Seeing the girl would only get me in this mess deeper. *Too late.*

The wallet was made of nice leather, but it had worn around the edges. He obviously used it a lot. The photo in the plastic envelope was of a beautiful girl. Blond hair, blue eyes—your typical little doll. Honestly, she was too pretty to have come from Will. At one time, my sister had had a crush on him; I never could understand why. His mouth was too big for his face, but I guess she liked his dirty blond hair. Blonds were rare where I grew up. But beyond his hair and his mouth, Will had some nose. It was so big that when we were kids, he got teased because he had to turn a pop can sideways before he could drink out of it. I handed back the wallet. "How'd you end up with her?"

He laughed. "She takes after her mother." Then his eyes seemed to change. They darkened while the pupils contracted and the lids drooped. He pulled out his cell phone, fiddling with it for a few seconds. Nothing could have prepared me for what I saw on that small screen.

"This is Lucy, this morning," he said.

The blond hair hung limp around her face. The blood vessels around the whites of her eyes appeared burst from pressure. Her skin had a strange yellow cast, almost like the color of an old bruise. Her face had thinned from the wallet photo. She looked...sunken. The basic facial features remained, but I could hardly tell it was the same little girl. My body grew cold again, like it had in the kitchen. This time, though, there was nothing to make a draft. The only window in the living room was the large picture one. It didn't open. I rubbed my arms. "What the hell happened?"

He clasped the phone like a lifeline. "The house."

My brows rose. I tried to think if any abuse could cause what I saw, but I came up short. The blood in her eyes occurred from some sort of internal pressure. Punches to the face could have caused intense bruising outside the eye and around the socket, but that wasn't what I saw in the picture. Scratches littered her face too, but they were thin, as if caused by her own fingernails. I was dumbfounded. What did he expect me to do? My body gradually warmed up again, but I'd had just about all the oddness I could take for one evening.

"Are you going to help her?" he asked.

Help her? She needed a doctor, not an ex-priest. "Will," I said. "How can I help her?"

"You know what to do." He sat motionless in that chair. Nothing, no part of his body moved. He didn't even blink.

I stood up and turned away from him. I couldn't face him to say the next part. I wasn't even sure he'd listen to reason. "She needs a doctor."

"Goddammit!" He grabbed me from behind and spun me around. His face burned red with intensity. His grip on my shoulder was so tight it hurt. "She's had a doctor! She's had twenty fucking doctors. She's been to internists, psychiatrists, PCP's, neurologists, and they all keep passing the buck."

I reached over and peeled his fingers from my shoulder. I wanted to beat the shit out of him for grabbing me and maybe knock some sense into him, but the man had clear stability issues. If something didn't give soon, he was going to have a nervous breakdown. "What do they all say?"

He threw himself into the recliner, the rage dissipating with his spirits. I had let the air out of his basketball. "The shrinks aren't sure what she has, maybe a split personality, or schizophrenia. I took her out of the last hospital because the quacks were considering electroshock therapy. ECT on a six-year-old! Jesus Christ." He put his head in his hands.

"Okay, I get it." I held up my hands and sunk into the sofa. "But what makes you think she's possessed?"

His voice came out in nothing but a whisper, yet the words had more impact that a five alarm fire, "Because she's not my little girl anymore."

Chapter Four

Tabby: Part 4

SOMETIMES, BEING A girl kind of sucked, especially when the mornings came too early. "Shit." I glanced at the window. The sun began to creep above the skyline. My insides churned like I'd eaten something that didn't sit right. The clock on the nightstand read six. A welcome relief. Class was hours away. I still had time to rest.

I rolled over and stared at the wall. It didn't matter how hard I tried, I couldn't shake the feeling in my stomach. It wasn't butterflies, and it sure as hell wasn't happy memories. It was more like a cramp, but those weren't quite due yet. I closed my eyes and tried to go back to sleep, but my brain wouldn't stop cycling around in my head.

"Screw it." I sat up, shook out my hair, threw back the covers, and got out of bed.

Scratching the sleep out of my eyes, I focused on the wall. What the hell was I going to do with this much time on my hands? I popped my back and stood. Reaching for an elastic off my nightstand, I pulled my hair up into a loose bun. Class wasn't until eleven, so I had time to work on my grading, but I would rather sleep than grade papers. Being a Ph.D. student stunk sometimes. Then again, it was better than working at McDonald's, trying to scrape my life together.

I strolled the hallway as my cat, Isaac, brushed against my legs. He was a Siamese with unusual habits. My mother had found him as a stray. A rare find to see a purebred wandering around with nowhere else to go. When I first saw him, he reminded me of Isaac Newton. Why, I didn't know.

I walked across the living room, turned on the lamp, and sat on the futon. Isaac trotted over and rubbed his fang on the back of my hand. I glanced around, trying to figure out what had me so uneasy, but I didn't see anything. The acid churned like I'd eaten a whole pizza. The only sound in the apartment was the ticking of the clock that hung above my television. I wiped my eyes again. It was too early.

I headed for the kitchen. Eyeing Isaac's empty bowl, I pulled the bag of food from under the counter and filled it up. Then I ambled over to the sink so I could get a glass of water. The sensation hit me like a brick. As soon as I had the glass in my hand, I spun around. *Dead.* Every plant on my table was dead. All the flowers had fallen off, and they drooped over their pots, brown with rot. Yet they'd been fine the night before.

Bad omen. There had been no reason for plants like those to die. I was descended from a long line of witches, and when plants died, it meant evil things were afoot. Sometimes, even the demonic. Until I knew what was going on, those plants were getting the hell out of my house. I seized a garbage bag from the pantry, loaded them all in, and unlocked the door to the deck. I put the plants out. When I left to go to class, I'd make use of the dumpster.

Thinking about the stench made me want to gag. I had a weak stomach anyway and this omen, or whatever-the-hell, wasn't going to make things any better. I walked back in the house and paused. I sniffed, but I only smelled my normal apartment scent—buttercream candles mixing with the Chinese food I'd had the night before. Nothing seemed out of the ordinary. Heading over to the altar, I clutched a sage bunch and lit it. It was best to do the cleansing now before anything else happened. From the looks of things, I was going to need all the help I could get.

Chapter Five

Jimmy

AFTER I'D GONE to my room to call my boss and get him to give me a leave of absence—not exactly an easy call—I headed back to Will. Without knowing how long this whole mess was going to play out, I'd figured it was probably the safest course of action. The stairs creaked as I descended. Will looked up from the recliner. I put up a hand before he could say anything. "Just a second."

Crossing the living room, I headed for the bookcase. Books upon books were crammed into every space. I began pulling some off the middle shelf. Last I remembered, I'd put the religion stuff on that shelf, but other tomes had long since been shuffled around. Finally, after moving about ten of them, I found my copy of the Roman Ritual. It had been buried underneath a Stephen King novel and a book of Thai cuisine. I snatched it, stacked the others so that they wouldn't fall on my feet, and shuffled over to my desk. I snagged a notepad and a pen, and then sat at the sofa.

"What are you doing?" Will asked.

I stared at his face. His eyes didn't appear to be hiding anything. "What is it you want for Lucy?"

"I want her to get better. She needs an exorcism."

I could understand having a child so sick that you no longer know what to do about it, but exorcism? What would drive him to even think about calling in a priest, let alone think his daughter was possessed? I kept my questions to myself. "If you're going to get an exorcism, you first have to convince me she's possessed. Then I have to look into the process."

His brows drew together. "You don't know how to do it?"

I chuckled. It never failed. Ever since the movie, *The Exorcist*, people thought that every Catholic priest could walk right up to anyone who seemed possessed and drive the demons out of them. Somehow, they never got that the story of *The Exorcist* was one of an exorcism gone awry. The priest died, and his assistant somehow got the demon to possess him and leave the little girl; then he promptly threw himself out the window. Not your rosy picture. "No, I don't know a thing about exorcism."

"Didn't you go to school to be a priest?" he asked.

"Yes." I resisted the eye roll. "Let me let you in on a little fact, Will. The church likes to sweep exorcism under the rug. In the past, there were many people who were thought to be possessed, but really had psychiatric disorders."

His face had turned red and his eyes bulged ever so slightly.

"I'm not saying that it can't happen, Will. I've just never seen it. More importantly, the only ones who really know a thing about exorcism are exorcists. The Vatican even has a school."

He glared at me, but his eyes pleaded. "Will you come with me to Sorrow's Point?"

I had a feeling this was coming. It had been the whole reason I'd asked for the time off. It didn't take a rocket scientist to figure out I was going to have to embark on this colossal mess of a journey. I knew where it was leading Will, but I had no idea what was in store for me. I grinned at him. I don't know why, but I did. "Thought you'd never ask."

He returned the smile.

I stretched my back. "Look, let's get some sleep. We can get our stuff together when we get up, and then we can try to figure out how to help Lucy."

He nodded.

"You can take the couch if you like."

He moved to the sofa and put his cell phone on the coffee table.

I brought him an extra blanket from the hall closet while he arranged the pillows, then crossed toward the lamp.

"Leave it on, please."

I dropped my hand from the switch and went upstairs, leaving the hall light on as well. It unnerved me to think he was afraid of the dark. The Will I'd known had been fearless; this new Will was…different.

#

The trip to Sorrow's Point was solemn and blessedly uneventful, but once we entered the sleepy town, I instantly knew what he was talking about. A strange heavy stillness laid over everything like a suffocating blanket. Homes lined the main street and had porch boxes with flowers in them; the whole effect reminded me of a wig trying to cover up a bald head. Even with the sun shining, the insides of the houses appeared too dark. The town looked nice, but there was something about it you couldn't put your finger on. A wrongness needing to rest. I didn't like it.

Will stopped the car. We were on a road that looked like it led to nowhere. Trees hovered over the road, an unnerving archway. The pavement was well maintained, but wet, as if from a recent rain.

"This is it," he said. "I'll understand if you want to back out now."

I glanced at him. "If I wasn't going to help, I would never have gotten in the car."

He nodded. "You can stay at the bed and breakfast or you can stay with us. It's your choice."

I wouldn't be able to live with it if there was something I could do for that kid. I'd stay at the house. So be it. "If I'm going to investigate this, really investigate it, then I need to be around her."

The path had a gentle grade to the left, and I found myself leaning in the car. He turned into a driveway I never would have seen unless I was looking for it. I would have expected a massive gate, proclaiming the house's existence, but there was none. It was almost as if the house wanted you to find it. My gut told me something was wrong about all of this. Granted, I sort of already knew that, but my prehistoric senses were kicking in now. I didn't have a lump, I had a lead weight. And sensing intelligence from an inanimate object factored right up there with possible possession. Creepy as hell.

When he pulled up in front of the house, I wasn't prepared for the sight. I kept expecting the grandmother from *Flowers in the Attic* to be staring at me through a tall window with her piercing gaze, but only curtains showed from the panes of the house. This was one of those mansions where the windows looked like eyes.

Will led me through the front door. It was even crazier inside than out. So much mahogany pervaded everything that my head swam a little. Mahogany staircase. Mahogany paneling. As far as I could see, everything was mahogany but the black and white checked marble floor. If this was the foyer, what the hell did the rest of the house look like?

"Tor, he's here," Will called.

Soon, a woman with the blondest hair I'd ever seen appeared from the back hall. I could see what Will meant when he said Lucy took after her mother. Her pale hair had a sparkle to it, and she had Elizabeth Taylor eyes. They couldn't be called anything but violet. She was slender and walked with class. Yes, there was no doubt about it. Will had married into a lot of money.

I held out my hand. "Jimmy Holiday."

She placed her palm gently in mine and shook. "Victoria Andersen. You may call me Tor. Mr. Holiday, I thank you for coming."

I glanced around the entryway. The massive mahogany staircase leading to the second floor was carved with intricate cupids and flowers. Old world craftsmanship. The checkered marble floor was even decked out in a diamond pattern. I was way out of place. "I don't know if I'll be any help, but I'll try."

She inclined her head. Unlike Will, she didn't seem to be so obsessed with everything. She wasn't jittery; she didn't have that wild look in her eyes that Will did. She was there, a normal mom that cared for her daughter. I couldn't fault that.

I followed them through the back hall. Will pointed out the living room, a powder room, and finally, led me to what could only be called "The Library." Mahogany overwhelmed the room once again. Here it was bookcases, wood panels, desks, and tables. Blue Persian carpets with a floral motif covered the floors. The room was roughly the size of the ground floor of a townhouse. Two large windows let in natural light. In various places, leather couches and chairs allowed for intimate conversation. A massive wooden desk centered the room as the main focal point.

"I think you'll be most comfortable here. You can't hear the noises quite so much in this part of the house," he said.

"What noises?" I asked, although I really did want to know. If there was some sort of tapping sound, a tree could be close to the house accounting for it. I'd have to check if that was the case.

He nodded. "You'll see."

I held back a retort. Being cryptic led to lies and I had no time for liars. It was one of my major pet peeves. Here apparently was a very sick little girl. One parent seemed to be hell bent on an age old ritual, and the other seemed to tolerate her husband. I was walking in a field of landmines already.

After Will had me put my bag on one of the couches, I followed him into the kitchen. Tor stood at the stove cooking. I didn't ask what it was, but I could tell it was Italian by the smell–some garlic, a bit of basil. Scents I could handle.

"Have a seat, Jim," she said, motioning toward the kitchen table.

It was one of those fancy glass tables with polished silver toned metal legs. The chairs matched with plush grey velvet cushions. I prayed to God that I wouldn't make a mess.

"We won't talk about any of this until tomorrow morning. The night is bad enough. I don't need it to be worse." Her hands gripped the counter as if struggling for composure. "Please don't make it worse."

I paused. She was much more stoic than Will. She didn't wear her emotions on her sleeve, and I could tell it hurt her to display these feelings in front of a stranger. She was used to an entirely different life, and either Will or something weird with her daughter, had turned that life upside down. I kind of felt sorry for her. Yet I wasn't sure why talking about it now would make any difference. Still, it was her house.

"That's fine," I said. "I'm here to help."

Apparently satisfied, her body visibly relaxed. She finished making dinner and served it to us, saying nothing. It was a quiet meal. Some sort of chicken with a red sauce and garlic bread. I couldn't complain. It had been a long time since I had a home cooked meal.

As she finished cleaning up, the sounds began: strange knocking in the walls, and something scurrying in the ceiling.

"We've had exterminators, carpenters, plumbers and engineers over here." Will waved his hand around the room. "They all say everything is normal, but they aren't here at night."

While not necessarily the sign of possession, the noises made my spine tingle. Knocking I could explain by bad pipes, but scurrying, not so much. "You don't have a pet?"

"Not," Tor played with a pendant at her neck, her mouth drooping into a frown, "Not now."

"And these happen every night?"

Will nodded. "Sometimes, and then for no reason at all, the noises stop. That's when other things start. It's hard to sleep."

Right now, it sounded like regular haunted house stuff, not demonic possession. But I'd yet to see Lucy. "When did the noises begin?"

Tor cleared her throat and sat at the table. "Let's not talk now. Talking about it gives it power."

That's when I heard the growl. It wasn't an animal per se, but it was odd, almost choppy. Completely unlike anything I had ever heard before.

"See," Tor said, letting go of her necklace. "Let's relax. I've already given Lucy her medicine."

"What about her dinner?" I asked.

Tor sighed. "She's been tube fed for about two months. At first, we had a nurse coming in everyday to check things, but that got too hard. The tube feeding, it's easier, and with her teeth, eating certain things is too difficult for her."

I wanted to know what had happened to her teeth, but I figured it would all come out in time. I was afraid for the little girl, and there was no doubt in my mind that *something* was going on.

After dinner and a blatant refusal of my request to see Lucy tonight, I went to bed. I made myself comfortable on the library sofa facing the door. For me, it felt safer to be able to see who was coming. Tor had given me a large afghan, and I had it draped over me. If it wasn't for the noises, I would have been at ease. But the strange sounds continued all night long in fits and starts. I would be deep asleep, relaxed, and then an odd noise would take over—a noise that even my subconscious couldn't ignore. Something was off about the house. I wasn't certain what, but I was going to find out.

"Yeah sure," I said aloud to the empty air. "Jimmy Holiday, old time cowboy coming to the rescue of a little damsel in distress." I snorted, sounding like an idiot. Finally, about five, the sounds stopped. Relief wasn't the word for it. I rolled over and drifted off. Then the dream began.

Wandering in a great forest, I put my hand in front of my face to orient the direction, but it was hard to see. The fog was so thick I could only make out the ground right in front of me. The trees, I only saw when I was right on top of them. It was like a forest of evergreens without the smell of pine. In fact, I couldn't smell anything.

Then I heard it, the strange choppy growl. I froze in place, not knowing if the sound was in front or behind me. Sweat trickled down my back, the fear turning my skin sticky.

"I don't think you want to go that way, mister." I heard a child's voice say.

"Why not?" I asked.

"Cause the soul eater lives there." Fingers grasped my shoulder.

I jerked awake.

Will pulled his hand back as if I'd shocked him. "You okay, Jimmy?"

I sat up, blinked the sleep out of my eyes, and took stock of the room. There was nothing out of place. Will stood over me. "Jesus Christ."

Will scratched at his head. "Guess I should have mentioned the dreams."

My jaw dropped. How could he keep that from me? I already told him it was important to tell me everything. It would have been nice to know that strange dreams had been happening to him. Then again, why would he assume that I would have one? Why would I have one? This already wasn't going well. "That's it," I said. "I told you that I've got to know everything. If you keep something from me one more time, I'm going home." Unreasonable? Maybe. But I was not letting it go. The dream still haunted me.

Will stepped back, his eyelids drooping. "Jimmy, don't. I'm sorry. I was hoping you would sleep. I didn't know if the dreams affected just me and Tor or not."

I wasn't sure if I bought his explanation, but it would have to do. "All right. Today, I want the whole story, but first, I want a shower. Then I want some breakfast. After that, we are going to talk."

#

I got my shower in Will and Tor's master bathroom. It was as crazy opulent as the rest of the house. Pink marble took over everything except for the gold faucets. Heat floated from the floor. I supposed that when it got really cold, having heated floors would come in handy, but what was the use of marble if it didn't act like marble?

I stood awkwardly in the bathroom, uncomfortable using the damn thing. It was too fancy for my taste. After the quickest shower ever, I wiped the stall and hung the towel on the rack to dry.

When I was finished with everything, I went downstairs to breakfast. It took me a couple of wrong turns, but eventually, I was able to find the kitchen again. Tor and Will were sitting at the table. Will was eating a muffin. Tor looked exhausted.

"Hello, Jim," Tor said. "I wasn't up to cooking this morning. I hope coffee and muffins are okay."

I smiled. "Lady, my usual breakfast is coffee and whatever I can scrape together. Believe me, muffins are fine."

She beamed. "What's the plan?"

Will grabbed her hand. "If he is going to help, he has to know everything, Tor. Otherwise, I don't know what else to do."

"But the last time—"

"What do you mean, the last time?" I asked. I couldn't not ask. Another lie of omission would have me hitting the roof. It was not instilling confidence in Will as far as I was concerned. So what if I hadn't brought my car? I was sure I could find a ride out of town one way or another. My thoughts were spinning.

Will sighed. "I went to the local priest first. It was he who recommended she go to the hospital."

I tapped my fingers on the table. "And this was the hospital that wanted to do shock treatments?"

"Yes," Tor said.

I was glad I didn't jump to conclusions and yell at him again, but Will needed to handle this better. There was no way the church would believe anything about the house, about Lucy, if he continued keeping secrets or omitting events, even if unintentionally. It all had to come out.

"I mean it this time, Will," I said. "No more secrets. You have no idea how difficult it is to prove possession to the church."

He stared me dead in the eyes. I knew mine had grown dark. They always did when I was angry, but they were a help. When my pupils enlarged and the irises went dark, people shut up and began to listen to what I had to say. My mother thought it was something magical. I had a more realistic view—my blue eyes looked darker when I held my head a certain way. I did this when I was angry. It gave a hell of an effect, one that had a logical explanation. That's what I had to do with Lucy, rule out all logical explanations surrounding her. If I had none, she was probably possessed. The chances of me finding no logical explanations for anything were very slim, and I was banking on science.

"What do you need?" Tor asked.

Now here was someone who had some sense. "Just my things. We can do this wherever you want." I got up from the table. "Give me a minute." I shuffled down the hall and into the library. Digging through my bag, I retrieved my notebook, a pen, and my Roman Ritual.

"I have a question," Tor said when I walked back into the room.

"Okay." I sat at the table and placed everything on top of it.

"If you think she's possessed… is there a chance you could do it?"

My brows pinched together. "Do what?"

"The exorcism."

Here we go again. I tried not to groan. It amazed me how little people understood about the Catholic Church. Technically, anyone could do an exorcism, whether it worked or not was another story. Not that exorcisms by priests always worked. The way I understood it was that in order to be an exorcist, you had to be pure of heart and mind. While I tried to be a good person, *pure* certainly wasn't a word I could call myself. But I guess it all depended on perception. I definitely wasn't pure of mind, but perhaps being pure of heart mattered more. That was really up to God. "If you want a church sanctioned exorcism, they will appoint an exorcist. I can assure you, I will not be on that list."

"Why not?" she asked.

I smiled then. "Because I'm not a priest. Not anymore."

"What if the church doesn't believe?" she asked.

"Well, I guess we'll figure that out if and when it happens." I arranged my things and turned to the section on exorcism in the Ritual. A list of things "proved" possession. I was supposed to disprove it. "So where shall we begin?"

Chapter Six

The Story

"WELL," WILL SAID, "I already told you about the town, but when Tor saw the house in person, she fell for it." He fingered his coffee mug and turned toward his wife. "I'll admit I was being a bit of an ass."

"When aren't you a bit of an ass?" Tor inched away from him. Definitely a place of conflict. That could possibly explain their bad dreams. My own, I didn't want to think about.

"What Will is trying to say is that I had already talked to Momma about the house. He wasn't real happy about it, but I didn't care. The house was to be my Christmas present."

I raised an eyebrow. "Who gets a house for Christmas?"

Will snorted. "The girl from Miracle on 34th Street and my wife."

Tor's eyes flashed. If Will wasn't careful, she was going to kill him.

I scratched my ear. "Anyways, so you got the house. What was it like?"

"Pretty much what you see now," Will said. "The furniture came with the house, and except for Lucy's bedroom and ours, the living room, and this table, we kept things as they were."

"The furniture was too lovely to get rid of," Tor said.

I nodded. From the tone in her voice, I could tell there was more to it than that. I really didn't care about the furniture, not if it didn't affect Lucy.

Will cleared his throat. "So we moved in roughly two weeks after closing. Lucy alternated between fear of living in a new place and bursting with energy."

"It got a little strange when we were unpacking." Tor stared into her coffee cup like it was a crystal ball about to give her a vision. "There is a huge attic. That's where we put the furniture we weren't going to use from Lucy's room. Lucy and I were looking around the attic while the movers were transferring furniture. She found this large old mirror. It was the strangest thing, oval with a tarnished gilt silver frame. The type you used to hang in a hallway. It would have been lovely with a little work, and if the looking glass hadn't been painted black."

Mirrors. Didn't it figure? There were old legends about mirrors. They were supposed to be doorways to other worlds. Something about the silver backing was meant to keep evil things from crossing over from the other side. What one painted in black meant, I had no idea. "That's a little unusual, isn't it?"

"Stranger is the fact that Lucy loved the mirror. She even begged me to allow her to put it in her room." She smoothed her hair back with her hand. "Needless to say, I refused. Everything was fine for a few weeks after that, and then Lucy started acting up. Sometimes, she was very mean. Not the Lucy we knew at all."

I was writing all of this as quickly as I could. It reminded me of taking notes in seminary, and like seminary, my scribbling was never fast enough. "So then what happened?"

She sighed. "We had a cat since it was a kitten—Miss Pretty. Lucy had picked her out." Tor got up from the table, took away our coffee mugs, and the muffins. She replaced it all with a soda for each of us.

I could see the strain in her face. Some memories will do that to you—the ones that make you look much older. I had one or two.

"I had left Lucy out back while I was in here doing dishes. She liked to play in the backyard." Her voice started to quiver.

I really hoped she wasn't going to cry. I hated crying. It was one of my bigger obstacles toward priesthood. Tears made me feel all uncomfortable and skitchy. I could understand it when someone died or something really horrible happened. But there were some people that cried over everything.

"I could look out the window and see her." She pointed to the window left of the table above the sink. "Lucy was supposed to stay where I could see her."

She sat, gripping her soda can so hard I was afraid it was going to explode. Her knuckles went white.

"Then I heard a growl. It was not Lucy's cry. The voice was different. It came from Miss Pretty." She swallowed hard. "I ran outside, over by the hedge. Lucy was standing there poking Miss Pretty with a stick. I asked her what she was doing. She didn't answer me. That was when I noticed that Miss Pretty wasn't moving and—"

She collapsed into sobs, her head lying on her crossed arms on the table. Will stroked her hair, and she sat up some and leaned on him. Her body heaved. It was a tenderness I didn't expect from them both given the way they'd acted earlier. I had a feeling that this back and forth could be affecting Lucy. Exactly how, I couldn't be sure, but a child could fake being sick because her parents were having problems. Then again, Lucy had killed a cat. Killing an animal was the sign of deep seeded mental problems. In my opinion, the priest had been right to refer them to a psychiatrist.

"Tor called me on my cell," Will said. "I'd gone to the store...can't remember why." His body stiffened. "Lucy had gouged out the cat's eyes, Jimmy. I...we didn't know what to do. Lucy seemed nonchalant about it. We knew she needed help, but we didn't know where to begin."

I squeezed my pen, scribbling questions marks on the paper. "That could be a lot of things—a brain tumor or even thyroid problems can cause mood changes, what they used to call multiple personality disorder—"

"That's what I thought at first too." He opened his soda and took a drink. "I buried Miss Pretty. Tor took Lucy upstairs and cleaned her up. She didn't speak to either one of us. When I asked Lucy why she hurt Miss Pretty, all I could get out of her was, 'Mr. Black showed me how.'"

I didn't know who the hell Mr. Black was, but the story rang oddly around in my head. I had that suffocating feeling again, the one I'd gotten when we drove through Sorrow's Point. "Any idea who Mr. Black is?"

Will nodded. "That's just it. There are two Mr. Blacks connected to this house. One long dead since the fifties, the other, well we bought the house from him."

I chewed at the inside of my cheek. It was a bad habit, but it helped me think. My dentist was going to squawk over it. I really didn't care. "So did you research the Black family?"

"At first I thought that the realtor was pulling a fast one or something, but after reading more about the house, that's when I started thinking Lucy might be possessed." Will cracked his knuckles and gently pushed Tor off him. She settled herself and wiped the rest of her tears away with a napkin.

"The house we're in actually has a name," he said. "It's called Blackmoor Hall. Black both because that was Archibald Black's surname, and for the black seam of coal running through the grounds. Moor because the land reminded him of the moors of Scotland, his homeland."

"And you found this out where?" As far as I knew, he

played with an Ouija board to get the information.

Will smirked. "The public library. The town is actually really proud of Blackmoor Hall, despite its dark history. Believe me, I wish we would have known about it before we bought it, but I guess it just happened that way."

"Or you could have used Google." I tried not to snark, but it was hard. Did I feel sorry for Lucy? Hell, yes. Did I feel sorry for Will about the house? Not so much. Sometimes it paid to do your homework.

"It's not on Google," Will said.

I arched a brow at him. "What do you mean? Everything is on the net these days."

Will shook his head. "Not the Blackmoor articles. The library hasn't gotten around to digitizing their microfiche library. At least that's the official line."

That explained it somewhat. "And the Black family?"

He chuckled. "Oh, they're on Google. General information about how the Black brothers made their fortunes in coal. The truth behind Archibald Black's death isn't online though."

"Interesting and odd," I said.

Will's shoulders hunched. "If Lucy wasn't involved, I'd probably write about it. As it is, I wouldn't have heard about it if I hadn't spoken to the librarian. When she found out I was the new owner of the 'Black House,' she said she couldn't keep the truth from me. She wasn't having that on her conscience."

Tor jumped up, went to a cabinet near her stove, and grabbed a cookbook. She began to flip through it. All of this really did freak her out. She was skittish like a rabbit. Maybe she had a reason to be scared.

"What I'm about to tell you is what keeps me up at night," Will said.

"Besides the noises?" I cocked my head.

"Yes, besides the noises. At any rate, when I went into the

library, I approached the front desk and asked the girl where I could find information about Blackmoor." He sighed. "It was like what you see in a movie. The whole library grew quiet. I kid you not. Then this little old lady walked over to me from behind the desk and told me to follow her. We went behind the circulation area and into a glass windowed room. She closed the door behind us."

His eyes glazed over with a faraway look as he took a drink of his soda. "She was a trip, telling me how the collection was delicate and that I could only touch the items while wearing gloves. I thought it was a little overkill, to be honest."

"Maybe we should call her for help?" Partially, I was joking, but I also had memories of grumpy old librarians when I was in school. Some of them, I'm sure, could scare a demon.

Will glared at me. "That's not funny."

"I didn't mean it to be. She knows all this town history; she might be able to help."

He exhaled a rough breath. "Anyways, I searched the room. She asked for my name, and I told her. She stared at me for several minutes, and then asked me if I had any children. I told her I had a daughter. Then she put her hand on her chest and went over to this wooden cabinet and opened it with a key. What she pulled out wasn't what I expected." He sucked in air. "It was a huge book filled with aging newsprint that was enclosed in some sort of acid free plastic. She motioned for me to sit at the desk, and I did. She put that book in front of me and flipped the pages until roughly the middle."

Will wiped at his mouth with the back of his hand.

"'Read 'til it stops talking about the Blacks,' she said. She gave me the impression that 'newcomers' aren't supposed to know this old history. She left the book with me anyway and exited the room."

I waited for him to continue as he seemed to gather his

thoughts.

"The first headline that jumped out at me was, 'Cannibal or Misunderstood Millionaire?' It went like that for pages after pages of text about Archibald Black and his obsession with the dark arts, his other misdeeds, and most of all, the events that led to his death."

"Wait a minute." I set my pen aside and stretched my fingers. I heard a crack. I was going to be lucky if I could even open my hands tomorrow.

"You okay?" Tor asked.

I nodded. "Cramp."

After a few minutes, the cramp abated. It had been too long since I'd written like that. I didn't want it on the computer though. Last thing I needed was to accidentally leak it and ruin Will's reputation. Not that computer work would really save my hands. Arthritis was arthritis. I was doomed. "Go on."

Will cleared his throat and took another drink. "Archibald Black didn't die under normal circumstances. According to the articles, there had been screams coming from the house all afternoon the day he died. Finally, a neighbor phoned the police. They knocked on the door, but no one answered it. After looking around the house, one of the men heard an odd thumping. They broke into the home and found Mr. Black sitting at the kitchen table, ripping the flesh from his six-year-old daughter's dismembered leg with his teeth. A young deputy, who had recently joined the force saw the scene and fired his weapon. His aim was true, hitting Black in the head. Black didn't drop the leg until he slumped over—dead."

He stared at me. "I practically ran out of there, Jimmy."

I tapped my pen on my teeth. "Doesn't it seem kind of bizarre and hokey that a random librarian would have these things no one else has, like there's some type of conspiracy?" If I didn't ask, I wouldn't be able to live with myself. It sounded too fantastic and too easy to be true.

Will said nothing, staring at the table.

The Blacks and their history provided him with an outlet for his denial about what was might be really wrong with Lucy. I hoped that wasn't the case, but I couldn't ignore the possibility. Then it hit me, what did Will do? It didn't seem like Will was the type of person to live off his wife's money, but this Will wasn't the same one I'd known for years. Why did he have the time to fret and worry about all of this? "What is it you do, Will?"

He looked me in the eye—hard, almost as if he was expecting a fight. "I'm a columnist."

That surprised me. Journalists were supposed to back up sources. Wouldn't he himself think this whole thing with the librarian was odd and convenient? It made no sense to me, other than the denial. More and more, that seemed to be possible rather than something supernatural going on.

"Don't feel bad," Tor said. "I thought it was stupid too. Until I explored the attic better."

I glanced at her. "What are you talking about?"

She smiled, but it was a cold smile. "It'd be easier to show you."

Without giving me a chance to respond, she jumped up from the table so fast I had to scramble to catch up to her. She led me to the dining room with its silk wallpaper and old landscape scenes. The massive mahogany table in the middle was large enough to seat twelve. Crossing the room, she opened a door and revealed a long set of steep spiral stairs.

"It's up there," she said, pointing at the staircase.

"You're not coming?"

She paused. "I've already seen as much as I care to."

It felt like a challenge. Was I really brave enough to go up there? Yes. I climbed the stairs. It was kind of claustrophobic, spiraling around upwards into the darkness. By the time I reached the top, I was seriously out of breath. "I need to walk more. This is ridiculous."

At the top of the stairs, another door was painted black and not as well cared for as the rest of the house. The paint cracked and flaked. I expected to have trouble with it, but it slid open easily.

I took a breath and peered inside.

Chapter Seven

Revelations

1950

THE MAN STOOD in the room, his room of power. In here, no one could touch him, feel him, or challenge him. In here, he was God.

He opened his hands and spoke the words the demon had told him the last time. Golden fire floated between his fingertips. It smelled hot and sulfuric, but his hands remained unharmed, as the dark one said they would be.

He picked up the small rodent from its cage. It squealed and struggled, trying to bite him. He let the fire travel over the animal. The creature burned. Its skin melted. Its eyeballs burst from the heat. He dropped the smoldering body to the table and grinned. His hands were still unharmed. The flames danced between his fingertips.

A sound broke his concentration, a child's laughter. The fire disappeared from between his hands.

Black threw open the door to his special room and walked over to the attic window. He peered into the yard. There they were: his wife, his daughter. The stupid cow was supposed to keep the spawn quiet when he was in his room working. That was the first rule he'd set when she asked him for a child.

He opened the window and yelled to her, "Glenna, are you forgetting something?"

His wife put her hand over her mouth and let the spawn back into the house. It was time he was rougher with her. Through pain, she would know his power, and learn to respect him. They both would learn.

Chapter Eight

Ritual

Present

I WENT THROUGH the door, expecting a place caked in dust, but it wasn't. In fact, it was amazingly clean. Even the sheets covering the old furniture appeared spotless. I wandered around. The attic had an oak floor. With its plastered walls, it could have been used for other things than storage. Oak encompassed everything up here, and it was surprisingly light. The rest of the house was so dark because of all the mahogany. Windows lit up both sides of the attic. I breathed deeper and easier, standing in such a sunlit room.

Then, toward the back of the attic, a door stood out. This door, like the one leading to the stairs, was painted black but freshly done. I thought it was another staircase, but when I opened it, a foul pungent aroma hit me. Darkness invaded the room, even with the uncovered windows. Black paint coated the plastered walls. One large bookcase, which held a treasure trove of old books and silver goblets, took up a section. There were wooden wands with crystals attached to the ends by gilded wire and little wooden boxes with the names of herbs and minerals on them—all things that I recognized as having to do with magic.

The air felt heavy and something invisible pressed me down. While I saw nothing disturbing, the darkness and the cold were enough for me to know things had happened there that weren't natural. This wasn't melodrama. This was real, and it scared the ever loving shit out of me.

When I turned to leave, I spied the mirror Tor had described earlier. It was propped up against some boxes on the floor. She mentioned the glass of it had been painted black. She'd neglected to mention the scratches in the paint that looked suspiciously like those from a child's fingernails. I wrestled the mirror into my arms, closed the door to that room, and made my way back downstairs.

I found them waiting for me in the kitchen. When Tor saw me, she screamed.

Will jumped up and grabbed a hold of her.

"What?" I asked.

Tor made a strange sound like a low keen. "I don't like looking at that—thing," she said, pointing at the mirror.

I sat at the table and leaned the mirror against the chair next to me. "Why not?"

Will let go of Tor, and then walked over to the table and sat across from me. "We found it like that after Lucy killed Miss Pretty."

Tor began pulling things out of the pantry.

"Did you look at the back of the mirror?" Will asked.

"No." I shook my head. "It didn't occur to me."

Will snatched the thing and flipped it around so I could see. There was an old label on the back. The ink had faded to an odd brown color.

Cavētis Tēctus Prōdiora

"It's Latin," I said.

Will seemed a little more uneasy than before. "Do you

know what it means?"

I nodded. "Loosely, it means 'beware the hidden betrayer.'"

He set the mirror on the floor. "On a mirror, what does that mean?"

Tor dragged a few pots out of cabinets and began chopping vegetables, ignoring the rest of us.

I turned back to Will. "I don't know. Not yet. Do you know if the house has been exorcised before?"

Will swallowed hard. "I have no idea."

Tor coughed then looked down her nose at me. "Can we get that *thing* out of here, please?"

Will grabbed the mirror and took it out of the room. While he did so, something was buzzing at the back of my head, the properties of mirrors, how the ancients thought your soul could be trapped in one. Something about this house wasn't right.

When Will came back, Tor and I were sitting in silence at the table. She'd gotten whatever she was making simmering. She didn't say anything to me, so I did the same.

"What happened after the cat died?" I asked Will.

He clasped his hands together. "I knew it wasn't normal for a kid to kill their pet, especially not like that. Tor...she didn't want to think about it."

Tor's eyes snapped toward him. "Well, who wants to think their little girl—"

He took her hand. "I wasn't judging you. I was telling Jimmy how it happened."

He turned to me. "We started with the pediatrician. It was horrible, Lucy fought and screamed. We sent her for tests at the hospital. MRI, CAT scans, anything that would show a reason for her mood changes. The tests turned out normal. That was when we began the parade of psychiatrists. They thought so many things, different psychoses, schizophrenia, delusional disorder, one even thought she was on hallucinogens! Christ, could you imagine? They had no idea. I've already told you about the last hospital." ·

I nodded. "But what makes you think she's possessed, really? I mean there are tons of disorders out there that most people don't know about."

"Jimmy, it's the things she says. She says things that she couldn't know. I don't know how to explain it."

There was too much to absorb. It was time for me to get away. "Ever think about revisiting the librarian?"

#

When we got to the library, I was struck by how small it was. A simple two story building that looked like it had been designed in the sixties. It was covered in light colored concrete and some sort of tan stone decorative plaster. It was a squat and ugly rectangular building, but serviceable.

It had that usual library smell too—books and heat.

Will stepped up to the desk and motioned to an elderly lady who was doing something with a stack of books at the back. She had an older style bob cut like a gray Doris Day. She was stocky, but not fat. Not exactly my standard views of a librarian.

She looked up. "Mr. Andersen," she said. "How can I help you?"

He grinned. "I need to look at the papers again. And my friend and I have some questions."

She glanced at Will again and then at me. Her eyes narrowed. I was expecting her to throw us out, but she motioned to us and unlocked the glass door behind the circulation desk. Will entered first, I followed, and she locked the door behind us.

"Questions?" she asked. Her spine was rigid, straightening her posture like an arrow. Apparently, Will had told a state secret.

Will nodded. "My daughter…she seems to be affected by the house." He pointed at me. "My friend Jimmy is trying to help us. He used to be a priest."

Her eyes widened. I was kind of used to the reaction, being built more like a linebacker than a priest.

"You aren't one of *those* priests, are you?" she asked in a snooty tone.

I knew what she was referring to, the molestation scandals. "No, Ma'am, I left because of a very mundane reason." There was no way in hell I was giving her my life story. It wasn't any of her business, and where did she get off accusing me like that?

She wanted more, I could tell, but she didn't press any further.

"I want to see the papers that Will told me about, but I have a question. Do you know if the house was ever exorcised?"

There was a spark of life in her eyes. She motioned for us to sit at the table. Her demeanor changed on a dime. It was almost as if by mentioning the exorcism, she took me seriously and found me worthy of knowing what she knew. She leaned over and spoke so quietly it was hard to hear her.

"They did a lot of things after the murders. Priests, ministers, and all types were brought in. Nothing seemed to help. Until they found a spiritualist."

Now, I was intrigued. What would a spiritualist do that a priest couldn't? "Why are these papers here instead of the regular part of the library?"

She sat back in her chair and laughed. "Right after it happened the people of the time burned everything. They thought it was contagious or something. The papers here are the only ones we know of that are left. I wanted to get them digitized, but the director refused. I think they hope these papers will come up missing one day, but they'll be here as long as I am."

I nodded.

"Now, back to the Black House. I'm not saying witchcraft was used or any such thing, but the rumors I heard was that the spiritualist didn't try to get rid of him like the rest. Instead she trapped him."

A cold chill traveled straight through me. Goosebumps appeared on my skin. Mirrors. Silver. The scratched black paint. "Trapped him in what?"

"They never said."

She pulled out the papers for me to read. Will left the room with the librarian, and I dove into the articles. After a moment, my vision began to fade.

Chapter Nine

The Style of Pain

1950

BLACK STOMPED DOWN the massive wooden steps of the front hall. He checked his appearance in the mirror. His suit was impeccable, black, made of fine wool and tailored to him. He straightened his tie and turned around.

"Be quiet for daddy, honey," he heard his wife whisper. A normal person wouldn't have been able to hear her, but he had powers normal people did not.

He smiled and headed toward them. The kitchen was where she belonged, but by tonight, she'd learn what it meant to cross him.

Black paused in the doorway. His wife was fluttering around, trying to please him. Trying to get back in his good graces. If she wasn't so stupid, she'd realize that if she'd play by the rules, she wouldn't have to do anything extra to please him.

He coughed.

She froze. Slowly, she turned around to face him. Her eyes wide and her mouth gaping, but she didn't make a sound. He liked that.

"Come take your medicine, Glenna," he said.

Her lips began to tremble. "What…what about the baby?"

He smirked. "The baby will be waiting for you when you get back."

She swallowed hard, wiped her hands on her apron, bowed her head, and followed him out the door.

#

He kept the room in the basement; the dark room, the punishment room, her personal Hell. Glenna knew it well, too well. Each time she'd displeased her husband, she'd been brought to this room. Each time after, she hadn't been able to function for weeks. Each time, the more pain she experienced, the happier he seemed.

She stepped out of her clothes without a word and glanced at her husband. He motioned to the wall. She gulped. The wall was the worst of all. She tried to gather her resolve as she slunk to the wall, legs shaking, and placed her hands in position.

In no time at all, he fastened her wrists to the cuffs attached to the cement. She could feel his breath on the back of her neck.

She wanted to beg him, plead with him not to hurt her, but she knew better. It was best to keep quiet. Begging made him hurt her much worse.

A whoosh and a smack.

Her body shook with pain. She could feel the searing burn across her back, the blood dripping down her legs.

Whoosh. Smack.

This time, she cried out. She couldn't hold it back. Her stomach roiled.

He laughed.

Whoosh. Smack.

Her whole world went dark, black.

Chapter Ten

Trouble

WHEN WE RETURNED to the house, I didn't know what to do. The vision I'd had of the Blacks haunted me. I rubbed my temples as if I could somehow erase the nightmare. I wasn't like my ex, Tabby. I wasn't supernatural in the slightest. Now, I'd had dreams and visions connected to this damn house. The last one wouldn't leave me alone. It danced before my eyes as I had read the article in the library, overtaking my mind, and playing with me like a puppet. Worse, I still didn't know why Will thought I could help Lucy. Maybe it was the priest thing, but they'd already tried one, and that priest did the same thing I would have done…recommend a psychiatrist.

Even if the visions meant something supernatural, what could I do? If Mr. Black's ghost was trapped here, that would account for some of the weird things going on. God, my head ached and I was getting myself nowhere with all of the speculation.

I fisted my hands at my sides, determined to ignore the throbbing in my skull. I needed to get back to the basics. Will asked me to help Lucy. I needed to see her.

Will parked the car in the front drive rather than the back of the house where the garage was. I guess it was for my benefit, but I didn't ask. We came in the front door and took off our coats. Will hung them on the antique coat rack beside the door. "You wanna meet Lucy?"

"Yes," I said. I was trying to look at meeting Lucy like being introduced to any other child, but that picture of Lucy from Will's phone kept coming to mind. That picture....that picture stuck with me.

Will led me up the main stairway, and when we entered the hall, the cold hit me. I tried to remember the location of the attic in relation to Lucy's bedroom, but I wasn't sure. If the attic sat above Lucy's, there might be some bleed over. I sure as hell wouldn't want my daughter sleeping below a room that had once held black magic.

We stopped at the first door to the left. Will knocked and then opened it. "Hi Lucy."

I walked in behind him and spotted her. The picture on the phone failed to capture reality. A smell so foul, I had to force myself not to gag, permeated the air. It was the scent of rotting flesh and over ripe fruit. Yet I saw nothing that would account for it. On the off-white painted walls, nail holes faintly showed where pictures once hung. No toys cluttered the floors, nothing that made me think of anything but institutional.

"Lucy," Will said, "this is Jimmy. I knew him when I was a kid."

Lucy directed her horrid eyes toward me. Seeing the whites so full of blood turned my stomach. A slow rage bubbled inside me, urging me to hurt whatever had done that to her. I stared at those eyes carefully, scrutinizing the details. Definitely not contacts. It didn't hurt to be sure.

"Hi, Lucy," I said.

She snarled in a voice much too deep for a child. "What do you want, Priest?"

Even if she was very smart, her voice couldn't sound like that. You could tell from the tone and articulation of the words that you were not talking to a little girl, you were talking to something else. Still, I wondered. Did Will tell her I used to be a priest? I wasn't dressed as one. She'd have no reason to call me that. If he hadn't said anything, a six-year-old psychic was as scary to me as a possessed little girl. A little girl who could know things would be a hard child to raise, and difficult to keep people from exploiting her talent.

Suddenly, there was a noise, similar to great claws digging into the plaster and running across the ceiling. I followed the track of the invisible thing with my eyes. There were no marks on the ceiling.

I returned my focus to the little girl in the bed. "I'm here to check on you, Lucy. Your dad asked me to come."

A choppy growl burst from her throat. No. It wasn't quite a growl at all, but laughter.

Goosebumps rose on the skin of my arms, and I was glad I was wearing a long sleeved shirt. That way, she couldn't see.

Will cleared his throat. "We'll leave you to your rest, Lucy."

She smiled at me, bearing her rotten and broken teeth. "Don't you want to spend more time with me. Get to *know* me?"

I swallowed. Hard. "Of course I do, Lucy. But your dad is right. You need your rest."

She chuckled like a demon extra on an old heavy metal album. Then, picked up her hand and waved.

We had been dismissed.

As we were leaving, the ties on the bed caught my attention. When he closed the door behind us, I stopped. "How do you know if she needs something?"

"Baby monitor."

We headed downstairs and met up with Tor in the kitchen. She was pulling the pot pie out of the oven.

"I'm going to be here a while." I strummed my fingers

along the counter, trying to figure out how to say this. "Something's odd about this house. And Lucy isn't well. Does any nursing staff come to see her?"

Tor took a drink from a glass. "We used to have a nurse when Lucy was more docile, but since she attacked the nurse and the priest, we figured we'd better not risk it."

"How do you handle it all? Lucy's tube feeding, her medication?"

"I had the nurses at our local hospital teach me what to do. I can do it as good as they can now. If Lucy needs something more, we take her to the doctor right away."

"So, why exactly did you start tube feeding her?" My head started pounding again. There was too much going on with Lucy and the house and everything. If it wasn't for the fact my folks were alcoholics, I'd consider taking a drink.

Tor sighed. "You've seen her teeth?"

I nodded.

"She chewed on the walls, the bars on her bed. She chewed on everything until she broke all her teeth."

I swiped a hand through my hair and tried to focus. Then, I arranged my notes, and asked, "How would you describe Lucy's speaking voice?"

"Like any little girl's, I guess," Will said. "We have some home movies if you'd like to see how she used to be."

"That would be helpful." I paused, unsure what to ask next. It was difficult trying to figure out what information the church would want, and the hammer continuously pounding at my brain didn't help matters. "Tell me about what happened with the first priest."

Will's eyes turned distant. "It was before she was in the hospital, like I told you." He stared into the flower arrangement on the kitchen table. It appeared to be silk, some lilies, but not a cheap arrangement. "We were at our wit's end. No doctors were able to help her. Then, after talking to my mother on the phone one afternoon, she mentioned going to the church. Now, she didn't recommend exorcism, understand."

"So what did she say?"

"She reminded me that priests were also counselors, and maybe it wouldn't hurt to try. It wasn't bad advice, but not the right choice for Lucy." He wiped his face with his hands. "We'd finished with yet another round of doctors. None of them could tell us anything, they all kept saying psychiatry, even though Lucy had had three psychiatric diagnoses at this point. So I called the only Catholic Church here. It's a Roman Catholic church." He paused, as if waiting for me to do or say something. When I didn't, he pressed on.

"I called the church and was put through to Father John. He's a pretty young priest, honestly, in his early thirties. I explained I was having trouble getting a diagnosis for Lucy, that we'd exhausted medical options, and thought the church might be able to help. We made arrangements for him to stop by that afternoon. We hadn't started tying her hands yet. The self-mutilation was still pretty mild." He sighed.

I waited for him to continue and wrote *self-mutilation* in my notes.

"When Father John got here," Will said, "Lucy seemed anxious. Father pulled up a chair in her room and sat beside her bed. He'd barely asked a question before she jumped up and snatched him by the throat. She'd moved so fast we couldn't stop her. Somehow, her little body had too much strength. It took both Tor and I to get Lucy off him. After that, we started restraining her when there were visitors." His head hung limp from his body, as if he couldn't deal with the weight of it any longer.

"Father John recommended the hospital. I don't really

blame him. He probably didn't know what the hospital would do to Lucy."

"When did the subject of exorcism come up?" I asked.

"After the attack, I asked Father John about it before he left. He said he didn't believe in exorcism or demonic possession."

Another hurdle with the church. Demonic possession had been underplayed so much, many priests didn't believe in it anymore. I heard a small amount about it in seminary, but everyone treated it almost like a joke. While I imagined most people who believed themselves possessed were either full of it or insane, I also kept an open mind. Too many things science hadn't quite figured out yet. "I know you're desperate, but again, why exorcism?"

He slumped in the chair. "We've tried everything else. If it doesn't work, I'm afraid I'll lose her."

Tor patted Will on the shoulder.

I let what he'd told me percolate around my brain and I needed to do some checking. "Okay, I've got it all for now. I'm going to go into the library and do some research. Let me know if you need anything."

#

When I reached the library, I sat at the huge desk, arranged my notes and opened my copy of the Roman Ritual to the section on exorcism. I had a set of twenty-one instructions that needed to be met before I could do anything. I already knew an exorcism needed to be approved by the bishop, so I skipped that and the part about the chosen priest needing to be schooled in exorcism. I rolled my eyes. "Fail there."

Section three contained useful information. First, I needed to exhaust all possibilities of something physical causing Lucy's condition. Second, Lucy needed to speak or understand languages she could have no way of knowing. Third, she needed to demonstrate knowledge of hidden things. Finally, she needed to exhibit strength beyond her age and condition. This was going to take a while.

I flipped through the rest of the section, which dealt with carrying out the exorcism itself. It didn't apply to me. But a nagging feeling wouldn't leave me alone. It dug into my brain like the blade from a madman's skull saw. I tried to push it aside. I wanted to ignore that room in the attic. I wanted to ignore the mirror. And above all, I wanted to ignore Lucy. Her abnormal face, her bloodied eyes haunted my waking dreams. And then, the still unanswered question. How did she know I had been a priest?

I left the library and went down the hall in search of Will. I found him in the massively white living room. The mahogany paneling either had been taken out of the room, or was never present to begin with. Everything in here read white, ultra-modern, clean. This, I could tell, was Will's room.

"Hey, Will," I said. "Can I see one of those home movies?"

Will's eyes darkened, but he said, "Sure."

He popped a DVD in the player as I sat on the couch. "This is last Christmas."

The screen filled with a beautiful Christmas scene, a large tree with multicolored lights topped with a golden angel. A cream-colored wall provided the perfect neutral backdrop to highlight the tree. Surrounding the bottom of it were numerous presents, some big, some small, but all ornately wrapped.

"Tor likes wrapping presents," Will said.

I grinned at him. "I can tell."

A giggle like a bell added to the coziness. Lucy appeared on the screen. Her blond hair was messy, but from sleep, not illness. She wore a red plaid nightgown.

"Daddy!" she said with another tinkling giggle. "I wanna

open presents."

Will chuckled behind the camera.

Tor came into view. "I don't know why you have to film everything. I'm not even dressed."

"Oh come on, Tor. I like to preserve things," Will said, off screen.

"Well, at least let your daughter open her presents."

The rest of the video revealed more of the same. Lucy unwrapped all her gifts, complete squeals of delight at everything. A solid black cat played amongst the torn paper around the floor.

This was not the same Lucy as the one upstairs, and for the first time, I let myself really believe, deep down that something supernatural had taken Lucy.

Will stepped out of the room when the movie ended. I could hear him in the hallway. I stayed where I was to let him have his privacy.

Women never seemed to understand that about men, I mused as I let the screen turn to snow. A lot of men cried in private. It wasn't so much about being ashamed, more about being protectors and showing weakness was never a good idea. Granted, dumb prehistoric bullshit, but one of the few instincts the human race had left.

Of course this train of thought got me thinking about the last time I'd cried—when Tabby and I broke up. Even though it'd been mutual, I knew I'd been a dumbass and if I'd paid more attention, we'd probably still be together. Even now, I couldn't imagine a girl more perfect for me. She taught me to live and be comfortable in my own skin.

The irony, and what would have made the church a lot harder on me if they had known, was that Tabby was a witch. Not the ride on the broom sort of witch, mind you, but a goddess fearing pagan. Of course, there really wasn't any fear about it—except her magic scared the crap out of me. Maybe it was I who was goddess fearing and not Tabby?

My superiors would have branded her damned, but I knew better. She was one of the kindest people I had ever met. She tried her best to live a good life. I didn't care that she was different. I didn't understand the logic of the church. How could someone so kind and caring be damned? I never believed God as vengeful. Odd for a priest, maybe, but a few of us didn't feel the same way as the church.

I watched the snow drift on the screen, lost in my thoughts. If this all went to hell, I could call Tabby. She did have a lot more experience than I did with supernatural stuff. Not every day an ex-priest has a witch to call on. Maybe there was something at work, getting me involved with Lucy. Maybe there wasn't and I was getting dragged into this craziness by my idiotic brain. Either way, if things got out of hand, calling Tabby would be a good move. She would give me a kick in the ass if I needed it. Maybe she might even be able to help.

I sought out Will and Tor in the kitchen to tell them this change of plans. "How would the both of you feel about me bringing in a friend who might be able to help?"

"What sort of friend?" Tor asked, her gaze never leaving the cans she was arranging.

"My ex-girlfriend. She might be useful."

Tor snapped her eyes toward me. "And how would your ex-girlfriend help?"

I took a deep breath. "Because she's battled a demon once before."

It got so quiet you could hear a bat's whiskers twitch.

Then Tor straightened and put some cans in the pantry. "You really think she can help Lucy?"

I shrugged. "I think she can try."

Chapter Eleven

Tabby: Part ②

AS I HOPPED into my car, I almost expected it not to start because of all the weird stuff that had been happening. Even though I had dumped the ruined plants in the dumpster, I still didn't feel safe. Something was not right, but I couldn't put my finger on it. Cueing up my iPod, I cranked the volume on the car stereo. It was a Type O Negative day.

It probably was weird to have specific days set aside for music, but I'd always done it. If I didn't play the right music, things didn't work out. Almost like a transmission that was missing enough tines on the gears to sound off but could still shift. The beats rained in perfect rhythm to stave off the bad luck. Most people familiar with the band would feel their music was downright morbid, but when I looked underneath, it was all sarcasm and message. When I felt upset, it was the perfect thing to deaden the bad things in my head. I hated that I would never hear Peter's dark voice again. I drummed my fingers on the steering wheel. *Rest in peace, Peter Steele, wherever you are.*

Suddenly, I heard an upbeat beat in the background, completely counterpoint to the song.

"Oh shit, the phone."

I snatched my purse from the backseat while keeping my eyes on the road. The car swerved slightly. I rooted around with my hand. Locating the handle of my purse, I grabbed it and threw it onto the front passenger seat. I finally retrieved the phone.

"Yeah," I said.

"Tabby?"

Holy shit, it was *him*. The *him* that got away. The *him* I'd corrupted. My defrocked priest, Jimmy Holiday.

Taking a deep breath, I steadied my nerves and said, "Why, Jimmy. I thought you'd disappeared."

He laughed. "Nah, just stuck in a cubicle for way too long. You still witchy?"

I snorted. "Um, yeah. I was born a witch. I don't think that's going to change anytime soon."

"Good," he paused, "you wanna come to Virginia?"

What the hell? Maybe this was the wrongness I'd been sensing. Things were pretty bad if Jimmy Holiday was asking a witch for help. When we were dating, he avoided my work like the plague. Now he was asking for my help? My gut clenched. It hit me—whatever was happening with Jimmy had to be what caused my plants to die. There was a badness he had gotten himself involved in. I sensed it. If he wasn't careful, something this bad could kill him. "What's going on, Jimmy?"

He coughed. Classic stalling. "You got any experience with possession?"

My body went cold. I pulled into my space at the college. "Why?"

"I'm here in a town called Sorrow's Point." He chuckled. "I know, great name for a town." A lengthy silence ensued and for a moment I thought he'd hung up. "Anyway, I'm here trying to save a little girl."

"You didn't go all priesty on me again, did you?"

"Nope. Guy I knew from back home contacted me because I used to be a priest. He thinks his daughter is possessed.

I'm...," the air felt heavier and his breathing turned deeper over the line, "I'm starting to think it's possible."

Right then. Not your every day, average call at all. "How old is the little girl?"

"Six."

It was all I needed to hear. "Where in Virginia?"

Chapter Twelve

Acquaintance

I SET MY PHONE on the table. "She's on her way." My heart beat harder. I needed to keep my head on straight. "She has to drive from Morgantown."

"Morgantown?" Will asked.

I nodded. "Morgantown, West Virginia. It's where she lives now. She'll probably be here in five or six hours. She said she'd be in touch."

He stretched his arms overhead. "Good. We can use all the help we can get."

"Besides," I played with my soda can, letting the aluminum crackle in my fist, "if an exorcism is granted, they recommend a female be present." I glanced sideways at Tor. "I'm not sure you want to see your daughter's exorcism."

Her quick intake of breath and her hand flying against her mouth told me all I needed to know.

"I don't think I can take much more as it is," she said.

"It's settled then." I eyed Will, not certain if I should even ask. The state of him didn't bode well, but he was Lucy's father. "Do you want to be present?"

He paused. "I'd like to try."

Would he really be able to do it? I didn't know, but it was his choice to make. Anyway, the exorcism depended on the church. My job was to collect information and get proof. I gripped my notes. I had no proof toward anything, yet. I needed to get some soon, one way or the other.

Chapter Thirteen

Tabby: Part ③

AS SOON AS "Die With Me" came on the radio, I got all teary-eyed. Dammit. This was *our* song. Figured, Jimmy would throw himself into my life again just when I got my shit together. I wiped the tears away with my hand and refocused on the road ahead. Then I flipped to the next song on my iPod. No sense in getting myself all upset over nothing.

It was Jimmy's fault we'd broken up. But, if I was honest with myself, it was as much mine. I wanted him to be something he wasn't. I wanted to change him—my first mistake. I should have counted myself lucky for having a guy willing to upend his whole life for me. He would have taken a bullet for me if I'd needed him to, but that was also the problem. There were plenty of times when I could take care of myself. Jimmy tended to forget that.

And now, here I was rushing back into his life. Completely voluntarily. I needed my head examined.

Jimmy owed me for this. My Ph. D. was now on hold. Isaac was staying with a friend. I took a leave of absence. I knew Jimmy was only calling me because he had to. I couldn't imagine how the family must feel with their girl in such a state that the father became desperate enough to believe she was possessed. With the dead plants, the feeling in my gut, and the fact I was now on my way to Virginia, it didn't look good. At least I knew what all the omens were about.

I wished Jimmy had been calling me because he wanted to, not because he needed my witchy expertise, but I didn't want to get my hopes up.

I looked at the dashboard clock, a little after six. Time to get something to eat. Each time a roadside sign appeared, I hoped it was a food sign, but none came. First came gas, then came attractions, and finally, food.

An Olive Garden. Perfect. I turned off at the exit. The way I saw it, food with garlic was a necessity. Garlic had cleansing properties, and from what Jimmy described, I was going to need them.

Chapter Fourteen

Jimmy

AFTER DINNER, WE settled in the living room, Will in the chair, Tor and I on the sofa. Tor arranged it so I was sitting between them. We sat there, silent. I got the feeling they didn't entertain often, and that they almost never used the living room for other people besides Will.

"Does anyone sit with Lucy at night?" I asked.

Tor's expression was guarded. "Not usually. When the sounds start, she's asleep. When I look in on her, her eyes are closed and her breathing is steady. She's the only person able to rest through the noises."

Something about her words made me doubt Lucy was sleeping. Will played with his watch, twisting it around on his wrist as far as he could get it to go, then he'd twist it back. His wrist was turning red from the metal rubbing across his skin.

"She sleeps," Will said. "I checked to see if she was faking once, but she wasn't. She was fast asleep."

With all the supernatural stuff involved, it didn't seem plausible for her to be able to sleep through it. But I let it go. "So, whatever this is, it is causing havoc not only with Lucy, but throughout the house."

"I guess so," Tor said. "I mean, it's scary." She ran her fingers through the fringe on a pillow. It was some sort of mottled velvet with sparkles in the fabric.

"Well," I said. "Maybe Tabby will be able to help."

Granted, I hadn't done much except witness Lucy's oddities. Tor and Will hadn't been lying about their daughter's transformation. But I needed another set of eyes I could rely on. I could only read the Roman Ritual so many times. Tabby had always been good in unusual situations because of her ghost hunting. Plus, maybe she could be a buffer between my brain and my doubts.

"I hope so," Tor said. She looked away quickly, but not before I saw the tears forming in her eyes.

#

It was a long wait for Tabby to get there. Almost as soon as night fell, the noises started. Because it was winter, night fell pretty early, around six. It got me thinking again. Would a six-year-old really be asleep at six p.m.?

Suddenly, it sounded like something ripped a giant hole in the roof. I jerked and stared up at the ceiling. Of course, there was no sign of any damage.

"Have you ever tried waking Lucy up while the noises are going on?" I asked.

Will's eyes narrowed.

I waved my hand. "I'm not trying to say you haven't done anything, Will. I'm trying to figure it out. That's why you brought me here."

Will's face softened. "I'm sorry, Jimmy. I'm so used to getting ready to fight with doctors and everyone else."

"It's okay. But have you ever tried to wake Lucy up once the noises have started?"

"No."

"Let's see what happens then, huh?" There was no refusal. I took my chance before they changed their minds.

I felt like a fourteen-year-old dared to go into a haunted house. Will said he was too afraid to do it, and Tor didn't want to, so I climbed the stairs to Lucy's room alone. Somehow I wasn't freaked out. Not really. I mean, she was tied down for Christ's sake. It wasn't like she could hurt me. So far, I hadn't seen anything to make me want to run out of there screaming, and the only thing supernatural I'd experienced was that room. My dream could possibly be explained by other means, and the noises I was currently listening to, well…we'd soon see.

When I got to Lucy's door, I paused to see if I could hear anything coming from her room. Nothing. I knocked and opened it. Again, the smell hit me. It was stronger this time. I had to suppress the urge to gag. I reached over and felt along the wall. As soon as my palm landed on the switch, I flipped it. Lucy laid there in her bed, but her eyes were not closed.

She smiled at me like a snake getting ready to strike. "What do you want, Priest?"

Something small scrabbled across the floor. I couldn't see it, but I heard its claws.

"Nothing, Lucy," I said. "I came to check on you. Are you feeling okay?"

She laughed rough and broken. The sound seemed to travel to the ceiling and out through the rest of the house. "You like to feel things in this house, strange things, don't you?"

I nodded. "There's a lot strange here."

"You like to feel other things, don't you, Priest? You can feel me if you want." She raised her hips in a suggestive manner, not at all befitting her age.

I wanted to back up against the wall. This was so fucking wrong. "No, Lucy. Don't do that again."

She giggled and flopped her hips back on the bed.

"Go to sleep. I wanted to make sure you're all right."

She grinned again with her broken teeth and licked her lips

in a way that made my skin crawl. "I'll be fine if you untie my hands. I'll be really fine then."

I backed away from the bed. This was sick in so many ways. What had happened to my sister wasn't far from my mind. There was no way Lucy could know about that of course, but it didn't help the way I felt. Chills danced along my skin like a colony of ants after a soda can. "Not going to happen. Why don't you try to rest?"

I had to be careful of what I said. I didn't need to give her anything she could use against me. It was too easy for people to accuse priests of molestation with all the cases out there. When I had been one, I had been overly careful that nothing I did or said could lead anyone to that conclusion. And well, me being defrocked meant that people assumed it had been because of that versus anything normal. Thanks media.

"I'll rest better when you are a part of me," she winked.

My body stiffened. The way she'd said it, that part wasn't sexual. She was implying more. Like my soul. I coughed and stepped out into the doorway, turned off the light and closed the door. I was torn with what to tell Will and Tor. Part of me wanted Lucy examined for possible sexual abuse, part of me wanted to investigate further. Sexual abuse didn't feel right somehow, not as an answer, but I couldn't ignore the fact that Lucy shouldn't be sexual at six. She also shouldn't even know what she knew about sex at six.

I couldn't withhold anything from her parents. I didn't want to tell them, but I knew I had no choice.

I took the steps slowly, one at a time, half steps if I could, trying to figure out how to approach this. My mind rebelled at the thought. I found them in the living room where I'd left them. Without any lead up or any chance to think, I stumbled into it. "Lucy wasn't asleep."

Will sat up in the chair. His eyes widened in surprise. "She wasn't?"

I crossed the room and sat on the couch. "No."

"The noises never stopped," Tor said, almost accusingly. She put her hand over her mouth and made a sound similar to a squeal.

I tapped my chin with my fingers, opting for a different tactic. "This incident at Lucy's daycare, you never said what it was."

Will sighed. "A male caretaker molested some kids. We had Lucy checked. He didn't touch her."

"Are you sure?" If I had hackles, they'd have risen now.

"The doctors said she hadn't been touched," Tor said.

"And you asked her?" I turned my head and stared at them both.

"She said no." Will wrung his hands together.

I sat back in on the sofa. The puzzle pieces started to fall into place. "She definitely needs some psychiatric help, possessed or not."

"Why?" Tor asked.

I groaned. "Because she came on to me. That and the way she spoke to me. It wasn't normal." Hearsay, even eyewitness testimony like what I'd experienced upstairs wouldn't cut it. We needed more. "We need to start videotaping conversations with her."

"What? Why?" Will set his soda on the coffee table, almost dropping it.

"The things we're looking for, they're going to come out in what she says and does while we're with her. Recording everything is our best recourse in documentation when we go to the church."

The doorbell rang, interrupting all conversation. One word escaped my lips, "Tabby."

#

I walked into the hallway in time to see Will let Tabby inside. She looked as I remembered, with her long red hair twirled up on the back of her head. Her pale skin flushed pink from the cold, and her green eyes were glassy with circles under them.

"Jimmy," she called as she ran over and hugged me. She smelled of something flowery as she always had.

I sniffed her. "I missed you, Tabby-cat."

"I missed you too."

The choppy laughter rattled the ceiling.

Tabby jumped back. "What the fuck was that?"

"Oh," I let loose a sarcastic laugh, although the hairs on my arms stood on end. "That's Lucy saying Hello."

"You're kidding, right?"

I shook my head. "Nope." I glanced past Tabby and saw Tor and Will standing there, watching. I coughed. "I'm sorry, Will, Tor, this is Tabby."

Tabby glanced at the ceiling for a moment then she squared her shoulders, came over, and shook their hands.

Will picked up Tabby's suitcase. It was one of those older models without wheels. As far as I knew, she'd always had it. It was a faded olive green with a hard case.

"If you don't mind," Will said. "You can share the library with Jimmy."

Tabby looked at me, a question in her eyes. "When do I get to see her?"

"Tomorrow. The activity is worse at night," I said. I turned to Will, waiting for him to say something, but he didn't. "The noises are quieter in the library."

"Lucy's noises?" she asked.

I nodded. We followed Will into the library.

"This is some place, huh?" she asked me.

"You haven't seen the half of it."

We set Tabby's suitcase next to the other sofa—the one that wasn't facing the door.

"Did you eat?" Tor asked Tabby from the doorway.

Tabby turned and smiled. "Yeah, I stopped on the way."

Tor nodded. "Are you tired?"

"Not yet, I'm not," Tabby said.

But she'd lied. The darkness under her eyes really stood out against her pale skin. I said nothing.

Tor ushered us all into the kitchen. "I'm making hot chocolate," she said. "Then, I think Tabby needs to know why she's here."

Chapter Fifteen

Investigations

I WOKE UP WITH a particular smell in my nose, the aroma of sunshine and quiet. I'm sure people would think me strange I say I can smell quiet, but I can. For me, it smells like Tabby's perfume and the scent of her hair.

Catching Tabby up to things last night didn't take long. Once we were done, the tiredness had really started to set in. Noises or not, she fell asleep quickly. She was still sleeping now, her arm tucked under her head. She always looked so innocent in the mornings. I didn't realize how much I'd missed her. No, that was the lie I told myself to make our breakup easier. I missed her from the moment she left me. I missed her goodness, and her reactions to my boneheaded stunts. I wasn't being sappy, at least I didn't think so. I couldn't shake the feeling I was stupid for screwing things up with her.

I couldn't even say there was any one event that ended it. Yet what I'd figured out over the years was I didn't appreciate her enough and I was an idiot. She was better off without me. I knew that. It was hard to admit to it sometimes.

After a bit, her eyes popped open, and she stared at me. "What are you looking at?"

I snorted. "You."

She rolled her eyes. "I should punch you or something."

I shook my head. "Nope. No punching allowed. Why don't we leave all the negative stuff in the past, huh? At least until we get this under control."

She sat up and brushed her hair out of her way. "I don't think this is something you can control."

She was right. "Probably not. Truce?"

A minute passed without a word, her staring at me all the while. "All right. Though, I have to point out I'm not even mad at you right now."

"Okay. I'll shut up then."

"Good idea." She snorted. "So what do we do now?"

I felt my face grow red. Good one, Jimmy. Real Smooth. "First, I want you to check out that room upstairs, and then see what you think about the mirror up there. I also think it would be a good idea for you to meet Lucy in person, and tell me your impressions."

Tabby nodded and headed for the bathroom. Soon as she was done with her shower, I rushed through mine. When I finished, I stood in the doorway and watched her for a minute. She was sitting on the bed, waiting.

"You ready?" she asked.

I shrugged. Time to try the "let's clear the air" thing again. Better this time. "I wanted to say I'm sorry."

"For what?"

"Everything."

"It isn't that easy, and you know it," she sighed, "but it's nice to hear you say it."

If it all was easy, I would have dragged her back home like a caveman a long time ago. Too bad it wasn't that simple. "So, we good?"

She snorted. "Jesus, Jimmy. I guess. What more do you want from me?"

"Truth?"

She nodded.

"Everything."

Her eyes went wide, but she didn't reply, just motioned with her hand toward the door. We dropped off our things in the library then headed to the kitchen.

Tor was leaning with her back against the stove. Bags hung under her eyes that hadn't been there the day before.

"How's Lucy?" I asked.

She looked at me, her nose red. "I think she needs a doctor."

It didn't take me by surprise given Lucy's condition. "Do you need Tabby and I to do anything?"

Tor sniffled. "Go ahead and do what you'd planned. Will is readying Lucy so we can take her to the emergency room."

"What do you think is wrong?" Tabby asked.

"I don't know what it is," Tor said.

#

Tor went outside to get the car while Will raced upstairs to get Lucy. I waited by the front door to hold it open so they could get her into the car easier.

"Do you think she's going to be okay?" Tabby asked.

I shrugged "I have no idea. She isn't well."

Will came downstairs carrying Lucy bundled up, almost like a mummy. As they passed, I caught a glimpse of one of her eyes watching me. She never made a sound except for breathing heavily.

Tabby and I observed from the doorway as they got Lucy into the car.

"What happened to her eyes?" Tabby asked.

"I don't know." Heck, life would be a lot easier if I did know.

Tabby and I returned to the library and sat on our

respective sofas.

"Jesus Christ," Tabby said. "What a mess."

I chuckled uncomfortably. "You're telling me? I really don't know what's going on. I wish I did."

She paused for a moment. "Tell me about this room."

"Freakiest place I've been in a while, that's for sure."

"How so?" she asked.

"I think you need to see it. I doubt my descriptions will do it justice."

Her brow rose.

"No, really. Get your witchy stuff and let's see what you can do."

Tabby laughed. "My witchy stuff? You never change, do you?"

As we made our way through the house, an oppressive sensation took hold of me. My windpipe narrowed, an invisible force grabbing onto it and squeezing. I cleared my throat. "It's up here."

Tabby followed me up the staircase into the attic. When she stepped in, she looked like a little kid dying to explore. We wandered along, Tabby peering under sheets, until we reached the other side of the house. I didn't have to tell her where the room was. She walked straight to it…and froze, literally in front of the door, almost as if a string had pulled her there and had gotten stuck.

"I see what you mean," she said.

I let her do her thing. She pulled out a bundle of sage from her bag and lit it. Then, she opened the door to the room. She paused again when she stepped over the threshold. A gust of cool wind blew, making her hair fly around her face. She began chanting and moving the sage around. At first, it seemed like nothing was happening, but then her sage stopped burning. No smoke, nothing. It just stopped.

"I've never had that happen before."

I scratched my head. "Maybe it's trying to keep you from cleansing it."

Tabby pulled a lighter out of her pocket and tried to relight the sage, but it wouldn't catch. When she flicked the lighter, the fire would appear, but as soon as it got near the sage, the flame would go out again. She growled.

"All right," she said, staring out of the room. "If it doesn't want me cleansing it. I'll do something else."

Tabby stepped out of the room and closed the door. Then, she started walking toward the other side of the house, so I grabbed her by the shoulder.

"Did you see the mirror?" I asked, pointing at it.

"Oh my God," she said.

"What?" I asked.

She crouched and turned it over. "Do you know what this is?"

I tried not to be stupid. "Well, it's a mirror…"

She swatted me on the leg with her hand.

"Ow."

Ignoring my distress, she continued, "It's much more than that. It's an old mirror. It's silver backed."

"So?"

"So!" She stood up. "So! You see the black paint?"

"Yeah."

"This mirror was a receptacle."

I leaned over and inspected the mirror again. "What do you mean?"

"Spirits, demons, whatever can be trapped in a mirror, but they can only be trapped in a silver backed mirror."

"Why does it matter?"

Tabby put her hands on her hips. "Because silver has purifying properties, that's why. It is an ancient thing because it's an element. Silver has been used to fight evil for a long time. Only a very powerful witch could have done this."

I really had no idea what she was talking about. "You mean like a spiritualist?"

"No, I mean a witch." Tabby cocked her head at me. "Who told you about a spiritualist?"

"You won't believe me," I said.

"Out with it." She tapped her foot, clearly willing to wait until I caved.

"The town librarian."

Chapter Sixteen

Trial

1950

O'DELL STOOD IN the foyer of Blackmoor. He hated being there, hated the feeling of the whole damn place. Ever since Jones had killed Black, reports of strange things going on in the house came to his office near daily. The Black brother wanted to sell the house, but wouldn't step foot in the place. He left it all up to O'Dell. Living in a small town, O'Dell never minded wearing many hats. Running the library was easy, being sheriff was his passion, but trying to get this place ready to be sold...that was a nightmare. The young Mr. Black had made it perfectly clear, if he didn't get the house presentable—meaning get rid of the evil inside it—he was done. If O'Dell didn't take care of this, he knew he'd be out of a job...all of them.

Finally, he saw a black Ford pull into the drive. She was the last resort. The minister couldn't do anything about the feel of the house. The priest had tried to exorcise whatever evil resided inside, but had a heart attack during the ritual. Another priest died trying to fix the damn thing. It had taken some time, but he'd found Eldora Williams, the most revered spiritualist in the country. She'd helped police from all over on a variety of cases—murders mostly. If she couldn't help, he didn't know what the hell to do.

He'd tried to get the other Black to burn the place to the ground, but Black wouldn't have it. O'Dell sighed. "If I can't fix it, let him live in the fucking thing."

Mrs. Williams got out of her car. Dressed in a large black mink coat with a hat to match, she opened the trunk of her car and pulled out a large black satchel.

He opened the front door of the house and waited.

She smiled at him, adjusted her hold on her bag, and came through the doorway. But, as soon as she crossed the threshold, she froze.

"A powerful spirit you've got here," she said in a voice that sounded like a croak.

O'Dell coughed. "Ma'am, I need you to move so I can close the door."

She looked at him, a puzzled expression on her face. Finally, she stepped aside.

He closed the door. Sniffing, she began walking toward the staircase.

"Wait, ma'am. Can I take your coat?"

She ignored him and headed up the stairs.

"Damn woman," he mumbled, but followed her. She didn't stop until she entered a bedroom in the east wing. The Blacks hadn't used it in years, the furniture covered in dusty sheets.

Mrs. Williams sniffed again then glanced upwards. "What's up there?"

O'Dell cleared his throat. "Attic. I think there's a storage room up there too."

She nodded. "Take me to it."

"We've got to go back down to reach the staircase to it." He took a deep breath. "You sure I can't take your coat?"

She shook her head and said again, "Take me to it."

O'Dell led her through the house and to the steps that led

to the attic. Once they got up, she practically knocked him over and darted toward the extra room.

Pointing at the door to the storage room, she whispered, "That's the heart."

His brow furrowed. "The heart of what?"

"Of the house, of course."

O'Dell watched her grab all types of things from her bag: candles and bottles of oils in enough colors to make his head swim, dried flowers and sticks of things he couldn't recognize, and even a few old iron nails. He'd never seen anything like it. With all of that in her arms, she entered that storage room. He stayed outside, staring anywhere but that room. No need to get involved more than he already had. The bumps and growls coming from inside only reiterated the fact that he'd made the right choice.

"Mr. O'Dell!" she screamed. "Go in my bag and bring me the mirror."

He raised his eyebrows, but said nothing. Grasping the large oval looking glass out of her bag, he crept over to the door. He took a deep breath, his heart pounding in his chest—*lub dub, lub dub*. He jerked the doorknob.

A huge black cloud filled the room, glowing with an eerie purplish brightness. The smell of the black formless fog drifted toward him. He gagged.

"Mr. O'Dell!"

He swung around and saw Mrs. Williams motioning to him. He handed her the mirror and could have sworn that out of the black mass eyes stared at him.

Backing out of the room, he closed the door behind him. He didn't care what she did, as long as she took care of that *thing*.

Chapter Seventeen

To Begin is to Try

Present

TABBY LET LOOSE an uneasy laugh. "Nothing here is normal, is it?"

"And think, you haven't even met Lucy yet."

"I know, Jimmy. I know." Tabby shook herself. "Okay, this is what we're going to do. If, and I mean if, Lucy is possessed, then we can recapture the demon in the mirror. If she isn't, we'll simply seal up this room and put the damn thing inside."

"Seal the room, you mean with wax?" I asked.

"Basically, and wards."

I could imagine how much of a mess that would be if and when we got the church involved. "Let's wait and see if Lucy meets the requirements for exorcism. That's what her dad wants anyway."

Tabby smiled. "All right, let the church decide, but here's a good question for you. What if the church washes its hands of the whole thing and Lucy really is possessed?"

She brought up a good point. The church would probably have notes from the local priest about his recommendation to the psychiatric hospital. If she really was possessed, the church would look at everything harder, and the church was anything but infallible.

"I guess if the church wants no part of it, we'll have to try ourselves—if Lucy's possessed."

"Isn't that dangerous?" she asked.

"Well, I figure we probably will be about on the same playing field. I mean, most of the priests who are the diocese exorcist in areas over here have never even performed an exorcism. It's a title in name only, at least that's what I read online." I paused for a minute, thinking. "So the way I see it, if they've never done an exorcism before and neither have we, then it's about the same odds." I ran my hands over my arms. It was cold near the room.

"You know," she said. "It's almost like an old joke, an exorcist and a witch walk into a bar..."

I chucked her lightly on the shoulder. "Shut up. Besides, I'm not an exorcist."

Tabby laughed at me. "Jimmy, I think from the moment you heard about all this, you've wanted to do it. Maybe you were meant to do this."

"And if it all goes bad?"

"Maybe that's meant to happen too."

I sighed. "I can't see how it's meant to happen for a little girl to die."

She frowned. "Jimmy, kids die every day, and this little girl is sick. It could happen."

I can't explain the feeling I got then. Some mix between trepidation and empowerment. "Then it's up to us to make sure it doesn't happen."

Tabby looked at me skeptically, but she said nothing, almost as if she wanted to avoid a fight. "Now what?"

I shrugged. "I guess we can go back downstairs and wait for news. I don't know what else to do."

Tabby grabbed another item from her bag. She began

writing all types of symbols on the door to the attic room with a piece of chalk. Her hand moved so furiously that I could see sweat running off her neck.

"There," she said. "That should help."

"What is it?"

She put the chalk back in her bag. "I warded this door to keep anything else from coming from the portal in that room."

"I thought we were waiting to see if Lucy really was possessed or not."

She snickered. "If the crap coming from that portal is what's causing Lucy's illness, I've solved your problem for you. If she's possessed, then what I did probably didn't do any good at all."

"Is the portal why the room felt so weird?"

Tabby smirked at me. "Yes, Jimmy."

She was being so condescending, but I didn't mind. When we were first together, she tried to teach me, but I wouldn't have any part of it. She had the right to lord it over me now.

"So," I said. "Do you think the original owner, Archibald Black, was possessed?"

Tabby stood and tapped her chin idly. "Well, it's possible, but there's also the possibility that his spirit's the one doing the possessing."

#

Later that evening, after Tabby and I made the most of delivery pizza, Will stormed into the kitchen through the back door.

"Jimmy, I'm sorry. I didn't know it was going to take this long." He threw his keys on the table so hard I was afraid the glass was going to break. He flung his coat on the floor.

I stood up, rushed over to him, and clutched him by the shoulders. "What the hell happened?"

He roared. I let him go and stepped back.

"I'll tell you what fucking happened, goddamn doctors." Sinking into a chair at the table, he seemed to collapse. I found him a soda in the refrigerator and set it in front of him.

"I'm tired of it," he said. "No more."

"All right, Will." I opened the pop tab and placed it back in front of him.

"I spent six-fucking-hours at the police station, wanna know why?"

It was Tabby who asked. "Why?"

He slammed his fist into the table. My empty soda fell over with a clang. "They, somebody, thought I was abusing my own daughter. Fuck!"

"Calm down," Tabby said. "You're going to hurt yourself." She placed her hand on his arm. That's all it took. Tabby was full of special gifts, and her ability to calm people was one of them. All it took was a touch, and Will's whole body visibly relaxed.

"Now why did they think Lucy was abused?" she asked.

Will took a sip of his soda. "Her eyes. It finally took Tor getting her PCP to fax over a note explaining the reason her eyes are the way they are." He wiped his hands over his face. "I guess some nursing student reported Lucy looked abused, and called the cops. The doctors didn't even know about it until I was already dragged to the station. Turns out it's severe oxygen failure, and those fuckers…" He collapsed into sobs.

"Is she going to be all right?" I asked.

Tabby handed him a napkin.

He swiped at his eyes. "For now, I think. They gave her a few things, got things going again. She's going to have to be on dialysis for a while."

I nodded. "So her kidneys too?"

"Yeah."

How much sicker could she get? "And her breathing's better?"

"Fluid in her chest, they had to do a chest tap to release the fluid."

"Jesus Christ," I said.

"Yeah." He wiped his eyes again with the napkin. "I don't want my little girl to die."

#

It was strange to go to sleep without a sound at all. At home, I was used to the cars passing by on the street next to my house, but with Lucy gone the sounds had ceased. The only noise I heard now was of the old house settling. Tabby and I stayed up late into the night talking—she on her couch, I on mine, but even she finally drifted off. I wasn't used to so much damn quiet. The last time I'd slept like this was when I was in seminary, and that drudged up some memories I'd rather forget.

My mind couldn't stop bowling over the same facts and events. I couldn't fault the hospital staff for questioning Will. Even I had wondered at first. Perhaps, for safety's sake, Will needed to put a security camera in Lucy's room so that she was monitored at all times. Then, if she did something to hurt herself, it would be recorded and Will would have something to back himself up with.

Plus, if there was an exorcism, the church would want video documentation anyways. It was standard practice now. I remembered hearing about a case in seminary where a priest was arrested for abusing the girl during the course of an exorcism. Now, I didn't know what the priest did, but if the movies were any indication, trauma was something that the possessed did to themselves. It could look like abuse, sure, but it was probably self-inflicted.

At last, my mind stopped spinning and I drifted off.

"Jimmy, wake up. I'm bored." Tabby woke me a little after eight.

From past experience I knew it was pointless to argue with her. She always had this unspoken rule—if she was up and couldn't sleep, those around her couldn't either. This impulse was one of the reasons we broke up in the first place. I still remembered times when I had a big project due the next day and she'd wake me up at three or four. Of course, after that, I couldn't get back to sleep. It was one of those things that got worse as time went on.

"Tabby, why do you have to do that?" I asked.

She shot me an obnoxious grin. "Cause it's fun to devil you."

I ran my hands through my hair. "You know, Tabby, there are times I really miss you, but not right now."

"Oh, come on, you know you love me," she said, batting her eyelashes at me.

I stared at her. "That's the problem. I do."

My utterance had a reaction from Tabby I wasn't anticipating. She kind of shivered then left the room. I didn't mean to unsettle her, and honestly, I hadn't meant to let that slip. We knew each other too well—knew what buttons to push. But it wasn't the buttons, we'd left a lot of things unresolved. I had to wonder if I was inviting more trouble by having her come. I hadn't thought about it before, but now, I knew I might have made a mistake.

Tabby went to shower while I searched out Will. An idea had hit me upside the head like a battering ram. I found him staring into his coffee mug in the kitchen. "We need to talk."

Will picked up his head, searching my face as if lost. "About what?"

"There's something that's been bothering me about the night you came to my house," I stared at him, pointedly.

"Something you said."

"About Lucy?" he asked.

"Yes."

"Okay." He wiped his upper lip.

"You told me the hospital wanted her gone after she almost gouged out a nurse's eye, but you said that you took her out of there when they were going to try shock treatment. So which is it, Will?" I drank my coffee, watching his face. "If she tried to gouge out a nurse's eye, wouldn't there be charges? Or at least a complaint from the nurse?"

He sat still, very still. "And if the nurse didn't press charges?"

"What do you mean?" My eyes narrowed.

"Lucy did try to gouge out the nurse's eye, but luckily only scratched the cornea before others pulled her away." He took a deep breath. "So we made a deal. Lucy's so young." His grip tightened on the mug. "Tor and I paid for the nurse's hospital bills. Luckily, her eye fully recovered. It was after the attack that the hospital considered ECT."

The answer satisfied my question, but it did nothing to ease my mind. Lucy could be psychotic. Odd cases happened where children killed. She could grow up to be a monster. That thought almost made possession preferable. "What if an exorcism isn't granted? Will, what are you going to do then?"

"I don't know," he said. "I honestly don't know."

#

Tabby appeared soon after Will left for the hospital. She didn't speak to me for a long time. She sat in her chair at the table. I sat in mine. The only break in the silence was the kicking on and off of the fan in the refrigerator. Finally, around noon, she asked me to join her outside. I didn't question it. I followed her, wandering around the grounds.

Underneath the snow, you could see the outlines of the hedges bordering each garden. Snow covered statues and fountains dotted the grounds. If it wasn't for the history of the house, I would say it was a stunning place, but somehow, beauty and evil didn't go hand in hand in my mind.

Outside, the house seemed normal, but I knew what lurked in the attic. Tabby froze at the edge of the woods surrounding the property.

"What's wrong, Tabby?" I asked.

"This isn't good."

I walked up to her. "What isn't good?"

"This," she pointed at my feet, "is a ley line."

"What?"

She smacked her head with her hand. "I forget how clueless you can be sometimes. A ley line is a power source, kind of like a grid, but a magical one. They're also doorways."

"To what?"

"To let things go, and to let things in."

I rolled my eyes. "I hate it when you talk in riddles."

She huffed. "Someone who can do magic can tap into the power source in the ley line and use it for magical purposes. Supposedly, very powerful practitioners can actually travel by way of them, but I've never seen anyone that strong. The bad side is the danger in ley lines. Dark beings can use them as doorways into our world."

"So what does this mean?"

She put her hands on her hips. "It means that Mr. Black was probably a very accomplished practitioner with a penchant for the dark side. Darth Vadar to your Han Solo."

I laughed. "If I'm Han Solo, who's Luke Skywalker?"

"Whoever can send this damn thing back from where it came from."

"Do you think it jumped the line? Or did Black invite it in?"

It was an honest question. I didn't have a clue.

"Right now," she said, "I don't know. But when Lucy comes back, we can ask it."

I shook my head. "Nope, bad idea. Demons are liars. We can ask it its name. We can ask it when it will leave, but we cannot ask it anything else."

"Why not?"

"Because the rules say so."

She snorted. "Jimmy Holiday, since when are you ever the sort to do anything by the rules?"

I smiled. "Never."

"Exactly my point."

#

Later that day, Will called to let us know Lucy was coming home. "The doctors figure since the worst is over and we have her feeding tube equipment here, we can probably manage her at home. I don't know if she was weak, or if she wanted back here, but she didn't act out or cause anything weird this time. Her organ failure has stopped. It happened suddenly." He paused. "So much of what's going on with Lucy is odd. They think that it's probably all right for her to leave the hospital since she appears to be stable. Honestly, I don't think they know what to think."

When Lucy came home, the house darkened. The walls and floors almost rippled for a moment and then righted. It was hard to explain, but without her, it felt like a normal house. With her, it was oppressive.

As Will came in with Lucy, there were no theatrics. She was bundled in a sheet with only her face peering out. Her yellowed skin and bloody eyes remained the same. She stared at me— hard—as Will passed by. She did nothing to prevent him from taking her back to her room.

With Lucy in bed, we sat at the kitchen table. None of us really said anything. It was tense and difficult when everyone felt awkward. None of us wanted to chit chat. We were waiting for something to happen. Finally, Will wandered in a few minutes later, a bleeding scratch on his hand.

"Got you, did she?" I asked.

"She always does when she's not restrained. I'm surprised she waited as long as she did."

"Maybe she didn't want to be restrained," Tabby said.

I glanced at her. "Maybe so."

After dinner, I figured it was time I brought up my idea. I wasn't sure if they'd go for it, but it was worth a shot. "Ever thought about installing a security camera?"

"You brought up something like that once before, didn't you?" Will asked.

"Yeah, for the exorcism."

"Well, we have a security system," Tor said.

"No." I threw up my hands. "I mean in Lucy's room."

Will looked at me, puzzled. "What are you talking about?"

"Think about it. If you record her, you have proof the injuries she causes are self-inflicted, then you'll be able to quell any accusations that might come up. Plus, the church, if they grant an exorcism, will want everything documented. These days, they use video."

Will tapped his fingers against his coffee mug. "It's something to think about."

"But what about Lucy's privacy?" Tor asked.

"She's six, what privacy does she need?" Will countered.

"What about when I bathe her?" she asked. "I sure don't want to record that."

"Well," I said. "You could cover the camera with a cloth. That way you'll have the audio portion proving that nothing bad happened, and you'll still be able to bathe her without invading

Lucy's privacy."

Tabby smiled at me.

"That might work," Will said. "I'll call around tomorrow and see what I can do."

Chapter Eighteen

Belief

THE SILENCE HAD to end sometime, I guess. Round about eight the noises started. At first, it was so quiet I barely noticed. Then sharp rapping came from inside the walls. Patters of little feet ran across the ceiling, interspersed with that same choppy laughter.

The antics kind of amused me in a weird way. I mean, come on, it was screwing with us. I should have been afraid. I wasn't. Of course, it wasn't funny at all with Lucy's life at stake, but there was a kind of perverse humor in it.

"I guess Lucy got out of her funk," I said, staring up at the library ceiling.

Tabby followed the sounds with her eyes as they traveled around the room. "It's amazing that all of this is coming from one little girl."

"Or a little girl who so happens to have spirits attached to her."

Will and Tor had gone to bed early. Their movements had been slow and their eyes drooped. Toward the end, Will could hardly keep his head up. So, it fell to Tabby and I to be the witnesses of Lucy's nightly antics.

After Tabby got tired of staring at the ceiling, she turned to me. "Do you think Lucy is in there somewhere, asleep?"

I shrugged. "Probably. Little as I know about it, from what I understand, when the demon is forward, the possessed is in a trance-like state. They don't even know what's going on. That is, people who are really possessed. People who aren't are just terrific liars."

"How much research have you done?" she asked.

"Tons. Every night you haven't been here, before I went to sleep, I surfed the net for information."

"Shame we can't wake Lucy up," Tabby said.

I smiled. "That's exactly what the rite of exorcism is supposed to do. It 'wakes up' the possessed and drives the demon out. Hopefully, to Hell."

"And if there is no Hell?" she asked.

I shrugged. "I guess that's what your mirror is for."

I slipped off my shoes and socks and stretched out on the sofa, propping my feet up on the coffee table.

"Are you ever afraid?" she asked.

"Sure," I said. "Wouldn't be human otherwise." The truth is, I'd been scared many times, mostly by losing people I cared about—Tabby included. "Are you scared?"

She nodded. "You know me. I don't touch the dark, never did. And this thing... it's nasty. It was bad enough I dealt with that demon as a kid."

"How did that happen?"

She sighed. "When I was about ten, a couple of friends and I were playing with an old Ouija board in the house. You know, usual sleepover type of thing." She rubbed her hands up and down her arms. "Like idiots, we'd waited until three. Since my mother had always told me three was the 'real' witching hour, I shared that with my friends. We figured we'd have the best luck contacting a spirit then."

Tabby scratched her leg and looked at her feet. "At first, nothing happened." She glanced up at me. "Then, the planchette began to move. We got spooked, so we pulled our hands away, but the planchette kept moving. It went faster and faster in a circular pattern around the board. And then, it stopped dead with the pointy part right at me."

She swallowed. I could tell that even now, it had terrified her.

"I felt something grab me and a bad odor filled the room. Things began to look almost brown—like I was looking through a dusty fog. I took a deep breath. Then, I heard voices. They were telling me all types of weird things. Some of them whispered to me to do violent things. I stood up and began calling the corners." A chill fell over the library as she spoke. "I hate to think what would have happened if my mother hadn't trained me in the arts."

"What happened to the thing?" I asked.

"I said some incantations for protection, and it disappeared. Luckily for me, it must have been a very weak demon, but I've never touched an Ouija board since."

"I don't blame you." I had heard the story before, but it was good to ask her to tell it again. Some of the things seemed similar to Lucy's situation. I put my hands behind my head. "Look at it this way. If we get the church involved, we probably won't even be active participants. They'd view us unworthy, I imagine, with me being defrocked and you being a witch."

She scratched her head. ""But that's what scares me. I have a bad feeling about all of this."

"What type of bad feeling?" I asked.

"That the church will refuse. Then, who's left to help Lucy? Me and you, and neither one of us know diddly squat about exorcism."

"At least you have experience with demons."

Tabby rolled her eyes. "One demon, and it was a weak one. Nothing like what's going on here."

I pulled my copy of the Roman Ritual from my bag. "I don't know if it matters, to be honest. In the early church, any Christian could do an exorcism. In the ritual, it clearly states that the exorcist must be pure in thought and intention. For both of us, all we want is for Lucy to be okay. To hell with the extra baggage. How much purer of a mindset can you get?"

"Is that even a word?"

"What?" I asked.

"Purer."

I chuckled. "I have no idea."

#

As we went to sleep, the noises of the house stayed with me a long time. Yet the scratching and pitter patter didn't bother me so much anymore. Will had said the sounds kept him and Tor up, but I didn't understand how that could be when I was getting used to them and I'd only been here a few days. Maybe they heard different sounds upstairs. Maybe the thing spoke to them through the baby monitor. I really didn't know. I fell asleep, figuring I would have more time to think about it tomorrow. Then, at about three, I heard it.

"Jimmy," it whispered.

I jerked awake and surveyed the room. Nothing. Whoever or whatever it was, it had spoken near my ear. Not creepy, just a loud whisper. But the notion that something tried to break through unsettled me.

I didn't bother going back to sleep.

The rest of the night the house was eerily silent. Even the settling noises of the house disappeared.

The next morning, I flailed when I woke. What I was dreaming, I couldn't remember. At some point, I must have fallen back to sleep. I uncurled my legs and groaned at the stiffness. Then, I felt something—a piece of paper clutched in my hand. I opened it. In a child's handwriting it said:

Liberaté mē

Liberate me. When does a six-year-old learn Latin? And how in the hell was she able to do this?

I stood up, walked out of the library, and headed straight to Lucy's room. It appeared almost normal. The early morning sunlight drifted in from the window. Lucy slept, at least I think she did. Her restraints were fastened to her wrists. The covers arranged around her comfortably. This was so far beyond what I knew how to manage. The impossible made possible. Granted, I'd read about people choking up nails during the course of an exorcism, things like that. But this wasn't part of an exorcism. This was from a dream. Now I had another mystery to solve.

Who wrote the note? And if it was Lucy, how in the hell did she do it? She'd been restrained at all times. Nothing about this made sense anymore, and I was starting to wonder if my mind was slowly cracking.

I left Lucy's room and headed back downstairs to the library. Tabby was sitting up on her sofa.

"Where were you?" she asked.

"I had a note," I said, but as I raised my hand to show it to her, the note was gone. Not in my hand. Not on the floor. Not on the sofa. I searched everywhere; it was nowhere. I ran out of the room and retraced my steps. Even in Lucy's room. The note had vanished.

I took the stairs easier this time around. No sense in rushing. Either I'd had the most vivid dream of my entire life, or someone was messing with me.

When I got back to the library, Tabby was standing inside the doorway. Her lips bent in a frown and her eyes searched my face. "Are you okay?"

I shrugged. "I have no idea."

"What's wrong?"

I sat on my sofa. "Either Lucy tried to contact me in a dream, by writing a note—in Latin no less—or someone here is playing a hell of a joke."

Tabby furrowed her brow and walked over to me. "That doesn't make any sense."

"Yeah. I know."

"Jimmy?" I heard Tor call from the hallway. I ran out. Tabby followed right behind me.

"What's wrong?" I asked.

Her face was strained. "Lucy... she..." she pointed upstairs.

I ran upstairs, Tabby following close behind. Lucy's back arched so far she was raising herself off the bed. Her eyes rolled back in her head so only the whites showed.

"Shit." I ran over to release the restraints. "Tabby, hurry, come help me!"

Tabby ran over and blocked her side of the bed to prevent Lucy from falling out. Tor watched from the doorway, her face lined with stress and the strain of it all. Lucy's back bowed so far I prayed she didn't hurt herself.

"Tor, has Lucy ever had a seizure before?" I asked.

She nodded. "Once in the mental hospital. They thought it might have been brought on by the medication."

I let go of the breath I'd been holding. "She's had CAT scans, right?"

Tor sighed. "She's had so many tests, but I know both the CAT scan and the MRI came out clear."

"Okay," I said.

Suddenly, Lucy completely relaxed. She focused those horrid eyes on me.

"Good morning, Priest," she said.

I grinned at her, as best I could. "Good morning, Lucy. You gave us quite a scare."

She opened her mouth to reveal her crooked grin and decrepit teeth. I realized then Lucy had spoken to me without her mouth. I took a step backwards. This was so very wrong. Her lips hadn't moved…at all. The sound had come from somewhere else.

I swallowed hard, stepped closer to her, and reattached the restraints to the bed. "Try to get some rest, Lucy. You might have to go back to the doctor."

She laughed a sound out of a horror film, all deep and wrong.

It wasn't until we were all downstairs and in the kitchen once more that I realized one of our party was missing. "Where's Will?"

Tor sighed. "He left early this morning to get some new prescriptions filled for Lucy. She's out of one of her morning medications."

Will had left early. He could have been the one to pull the note thing on me, but what would he accomplish by doing it? True, he could be insane enough to think it could help make me believe Lucy was possessed, not that I needed much convincing at this point. But it still didn't make any sense, which meant I still had no explanation for what had happened. "I think Lucy needs to be checked out again," I said. "Grand mal seizures aren't something to play around with."

Tor tucked her face in her hands. "When's it ever going to stop, Jimmy? When's my little girl going to be okay?"

I shook my head. "I don't know, Tor. I don't."

Chapter Nineteen

Medicine

GETTING LUCY INTO the car was no easy feat. Tor had called the doctor, and he wanted to see Lucy right away. All of Lucy's IV's and her feeding tube had to be unhooked. Then, Tor changed her nightgown and even before we took her out, Tabby had to be ready near the front door with the back door of her car open.

Will had come back just in time for Tor to explain what we were doing. He decided to go ahead and head out two hours to Costco for a video camera. I didn't mind helping Tor, I truly didn't, but there was part of me that wondered if Will should have been the one going to the doctor while Tabby and I tried to find a video camera. I envied him.

"Why the back seat?" I asked Tor as she carried Lucy downstairs.

"Because," she said, "if Lucy's upfront, she'll grab the wheel."

I nodded. "What about a car seat?"

Tor swallowed hard. "We stopped trying to get her in one. I'll deal with it if we get pulled over."

Lucy kept strangely silent. I don't know if she wanted to go for a car ride or if she wanted to see the doctor, but she said nothing.

During the drive, everything seemed calm…until we passed a church.

"Malenki Bog," Lucy said.

I spun around in the front seat to stare at her. Tor glanced at me, her eyes wide. The air inside the car grew cold. Goosebumps broke out along my skin.

"What did you say, Lucy?" I asked.

Tor stared at her daughter.

"Yevo Nyet."

"What honey?" Tor asked.

It was my luck. It figured, Lucy started speaking in different languages when I had no way to document her. I wished I knew what she was saying. It sounded like Russian.

Tabby kept glancing in the rear view mirror as she drove. Her mouth gaped open like a fish.

Then Lucy laughed, her head laying against her mother's chest. There was a pause as her head hung lower, her lips pulled into a frown. "Mnye ploho."

Frost started to form on the inside of the car windows.

Tabby pulled into the parking lot at the doctor's office, located in a small shopping center. The building was red brick with white wooden accents. The sign had federal style swirls on the top and bottom and read, "Wilbur Sine, MD."

"Wait here," Tor said. "It'll be easier. If I need anything, I'll call."

In this light, Lucy was nothing scary, just a little girl far too sick for her age. Her skin was pale, yet slightly yellow. Deep scratches surrounded her cheeks and forehead, most of which had healed. Her face appeared practically branded with lines of scars.

"Well, what do you think of that?" Tabby asked as Tor and Lucy disappeared into the doctor's office.

I sighed and rubbed my hands together. "I'm pissed cause

we had nothing to record her with. And I wish we could prove somehow what happened here." I pointed at the moisture in the inside of the windshield. "But I don't know if the language stuff would have been proof anyway."

"How come?"

I tapped my fingers on the dashboard. "Will's mother is Russian. I remember that from way back when. She could have taught Lucy some words."

Tabby stared at me. "I don't know, Jimmy. Her accent was too good. It was like a native speaker. I mean, my roommate took Russian in college. She used to practice in our doom room. I know what Russian is supposed to sound like, and she had it down cold. Didn't you say on the video you watched that Lucy sounded like a normal six-year-old?"

"Yeah."

"So," Tabby said. "How in the hell is a kid whose main language is English, and whose parents only speak English, able to deal with consonant clusters?"

I sighed. "It doesn't matter anyway. We didn't get it recorded."

"I really can't believe this. Finally, something happens that could be used, and you don't have your shit together to do much of anything."

"What do you mean?" I asked.

"You have a cell phone. I assume it takes video."

I chuckled at her. "Yeah, and cell phone videos are such reliable evidence."

She blinked. "They can be."

"Would you believe a cell phone video of a supposed possession?"

I didn't get an answer. She leaned back in her seat and stared out the window.

There was nothing I could do. I knew the church wouldn't

see it as proof. Lucy had to do something like speak biblical Greek for them to take the case seriously. Russian, would have been great, that is if Lucy didn't have a Russian grandmother.

It was disappointing. It wasn't that I thought I knew better, but it seemed like every time I got an idea, something was laughing at me, seriously wanting me to fail. If I knew what Lucy had said, it might have given me some clue as to where to turn, but I had no idea what she'd said. I really wished I spoke Russian.

#

About an hour later, Tor came out carrying Lucy. Lucy appeared to be sedated by the way she hung limply in Tor's arms.

"What did the doctor say?" Tabby asked.

Tor sighed. "That he would send in the paperwork for her to have another CAT scan. And if happens again, I'm supposed to take her to the emergency room. Thank God for good health insurance."

Tabby's hands tightened on the wheel and she never met my gaze as she drove. Still pissed. I guessed because I pointed out again something that she didn't want to face—that according to the church and many other people, we were unreliable sources. It wasn't my fault the church was so thorough. If the world was perfect, we wouldn't even be here.

When we got back, I helped Tor get Lucy into the house while Tabby parked her car around back. Hopefully, she'd calm soon. I was going to need her help.

"Hey, Tor?" I asked, sitting at the kitchen table.

"Yes, Jimmy?"

"Did Lucy's grandmother teach her any Russian?"

Tor turned around. "Honestly, Will's mother hasn't spoken Russian in so long, she's probably rusty. I'm almost positive she's taught Lucy nothing."

I nodded. "Just making sure."

She leaned her back against the counter. "What do you think, Jimmy, really?"

I'd been waiting for this question. I wasn't sure if I had the answer she wanted. "The truth is, I do think there's a spirit haunting Lucy. Whether it's a full possession, I don't know. But then, I wasn't supposed to know. When I was a priest, I was a regular parish priest, nothing special."

Her eyes teared up, but she said nothing.

Tabby came in through the back door, closing it quietly behind her, and ignoring me completely.

#

Finally, a little after five, Will showed up. He clumped into the house through the back door with bags and boxes, completely out of breath.

"What took so long?" Tor asked.

I jumped up from the table and helped Will with some of the packages. After we got everything into some sort of cohesive arrangement on the floor, Will threw himself into a kitchen chair.

"Costco didn't have the camera system. I ended up going to four different stores in order to get everything we need, and made a side trip to an AV repair place for instructions on how to set up the whole mess."

"Is it going to be hard?" I asked.

Will shrugged. "It's not supposed to be, but you know how those things always work out."

"Well, there are four of us. Maybe it really won't be so bad."

"I hope not."

Tor sighed. "Do I even want to know how much all this cost?"

"Probably not," Will said, an odd look in his eye.

Tor got up, served him a bowl of cabbage soup, and sat back at the table. She said nothing more.

Apparently, their distress was coming from more than one direction. I didn't want to pry, but it was hard hearing all of this. I was too close. Now I knew about their marital problems, and a hint of financial problems. I hoped the longer I stayed, they would realize they were letting me know things I shouldn't know, but somehow that seemed unlikely. Sometimes, I wondered if they forgot Tabby and I were even there.

Will ate in silence, but Tor and Will's body language spoke for them. Although they sat next to each other, they made sure not to touch. It was strange to watch, and I didn't want to, but something unwritten compelled me to anyway.

"Jimmy?" Will asked when Tor started doing the dishes.

"Yeah?"

"Want to help me get this set up?"

I got up from the table. Tabby followed. I figured she finally got tired of trying to stay mad at me. We dragged the boxes and bags upstairs. Lucy was eerily quiet. Not even a peep of the noises could be heard.

Once we got to her door, Will knocked and opened it. "Lucy, honey? We are going to hook up this stuff, and then we'll let you rest."

We all stepped into the room. Lucy watched us, her eyes following us around the room. Her face was still yellow and the scarring made her look like she was wrinkled in odd places. Being restrained allowed the scratches to heal, but the scars were still dark against her skin.

"Why not say what you mean, father?" Lucy gaped at him. "You are putting cameras in here to watch me, to see what I'll do."

Will paused. I could tell he was torn between knowing his

daughter was only six-years-old and this thing making her speak years older than she was.

"Yes, Lucy," he said. "We need to watch you."

"Why, want some kiddy fuckers to see me, daddy?"

Will's shoulders slumped. "Why don't you rest now?"

Lucy laughed, quietly and an octave lower.

It was bad. Really bad. If I had any doubts, I just heard more than enough to know she truly was possessed. Six-year-olds didn't talk like that.

It took over two hours to get the system running. When it was time to place the camera in the bracket and attach the cables, I volunteered to climb the ladder. Will was exhausted from the traveling he'd done all day, and Tabby, well, I didn't want her to deal with it.

"Tabby," I said. "Hold the camera, and I'll let you know when I'm ready for it."

She nodded. "It's under control, Jimmy."

"Okay, turn it on. Let's see if it works," I said.

As the wiring all went into place, something pushed me. I clutched the ladder—hard. Tabby screamed. The ladder tipped and swayed back and forth across the floor. I was caught on an insane teeter totter whose focus was to throw me off.

"Lucy, stop!" Will stood frozen in the middle of the floor, his body straining against invisible forces that held him motionless.

The ladder stopped moving.

"But, Daddy," it said, no longer Lucy. "I was having fun."

I got off the ladder, one wrung at a time. Lucy grinned at me. It was one of the scariest smiles I'd ever seen. Her bloody red eyes narrowed, and her lips pulled up too far on either side of her mouth, almost like a dog's mouth without a snout. At first the pupils of her eyes appeared to turn elliptical, like a snake's, but when I blinked, her eyes rounded, human again.

Bloody, but human. Her mouth, however, did not change.

"Father Holiday and I are good friends, aren't we?" she asked.

"If that's what you want to call it," I countered.

Then she laughed again. We left the room.

"Did you get all that?" Tabby asked.

Will grinned. "It might have scared the shit out of Jimmy, but yeah, I think I did."

He took a look at the DVR and made sure the green light indicating it was recording was still on. "Let's go see."

Chapter Twenty

Getting Stronger

TABBY AND I headed for the living room while Will went to the kitchen to check on Tor. My stomach roiled, still unsettled by Lucy's attack. Tabby, however, seemed unaffected. Then again, she didn't tend to show things outwardly. And since the threat was now gone, she had no reason to freak out. Knocking me off a ladder wouldn't have killed me, not from that height, so I was left wondering if the demon wanted to scare me.

Will entered alone.

"Where's Tor?" Tabby asked.

He coughed. "Tor says she's scared enough. She doesn't want to see it."

I nodded.

Will attached his laptop to the TV. While the video loaded, I peered over at Tabby. She seemed thoughtful.

The footage picked up as the ladder was teetering back and forth. I suppose that for the beginning of the attack, the machine must have been booting up.

I glanced over at Will. He stood in the doorway. "I think this is going to work."

Will smiled, but it was a sad smile. "It better for what I paid for it. What now?"

"Now that we have the video, starting tomorrow, Tabby

and I are going to spend more time with Lucy. If I can get the proof we need, I'll contact the church."

"That's it?" Will asked.

"That's all we can do."

#

I got an odd feeling in the middle of my sleep. I wasn't sure what was going on, but something felt awry, and not quite of this world. My eyes snapped open. I stared at the clock. Once again, I awoke at three. I glanced over at Tabby. She was still asleep, but her body tossed restlessly. Standing behind Tabby's sofa was an immense black hooded figure—at least seven feet tall. I couldn't see its face, but red eyes peered out from underneath the hood. Skeletal hands, no flesh on them at all, reached out.

My body froze, not only from fear, but the freezing air in the room. I didn't know if it had come through the ley line or if it had broken Tabby's wards on the room upstairs. Hell, maybe it was the physical manifestation of the thing possessing Lucy. I did know one thing for certain—I didn't want this thing hurting Tabby.

"The lord is my shepherd," I began.

The thing snarled. I couldn't see its face because of the hood, but something told me I didn't want to. It swung its hand at me. It didn't connect, but an invisible force did. A giant burst of energy seized hold of me and threw me into a chair across the room. The chair collapsed underneath me.

"Holy shit!"

My whole body hummed with pain, but I didn't have time for it. Hell, I didn't have time to breathe. I hobbled off the broken chair, knelt on my knees, and closed my eyes. I prayed to God to keep Tabby safe, prayed to send this thing back to where it came from.

A breath later, I opened my eyes. It hadn't moved. Anger outweighed fear, coursing in my blood, and pumping adrenaline through my veins. I turned my head up toward it. "Listen, you overgrown bag of bones. I didn't invite you here, and I sure as hell know Will and Victoria didn't invite you either, so get the fuck out of this house! Your invitation is revoked!"

I panted. One breath. Two. The thing disappeared with a loud bang. The room trembled. I hobbled over to Tabby and shook her awake.

She punched me in the eye.

"Damn it." That's what I needed, a black eye to match my other bruises. "What the hell was that for?"

"You lived with me for four years, Jimmy Holiday. You know better than to touch me to wake me." She sat up and rubbed her hand.

This was turning out to be a helluva night. Not only was I beaten up by a hooded demonic force, but I'd been punched in the eye by my ex-girlfriend. What was next, a house falling on me? Adrenaline raced through me. I knew I'd come down from it, but not now, not yet. I had to hold on to whatever strength remained in me.

"In case you're interested, a shadow person thing tried to eat your soul," I said, huffing.

"What?"

"You heard me." I took a moment to get my breath back. This had moved from bizarre to seriously screwed up. I mean shit, a skeletal demon figure? What the hell? Something inside me knew the answer. "A soul sucker."

Glancing around the room, her gaze zeroed on the broken chair. "It did that?"

I nodded.

"Jesus Christ."

"Nope," I shook my head, trying to lighten the mood. "Not

Jesus. Jimmy Fucking Holiday."

She stared at me like I'd grown about fourteen heads.

"You got anything to say?" I asked.

She raised her eyebrows, a smirk breaking across her lips. "You know you've given yourself at least ten years in Purgatory."

"Who told you about Purgatory?" I asked.

She lay back on the sofa and closed her eyes. After a moment, she opened one eye. "Purgatorians."

I got on my own couch and hunkered down. "Go to sleep."

She threw a pillow at me. "You go to sleep. I'm trying to rest."

"I'll shut up now."

"You do that."

#

Last night sucked. No bones about it. Everything that was happening had one thing in common—Lucy. Our moods were affected, the weird happenings like the note and the hooded beast thing, all of it was connected. And how did I know the hooded thing was a soul sucker? I'd never seen one. Hell, I only heard about them from that dream. It was like I'd been caught between two worlds.

My bruises ached. At least nothing was broken, but I still felt like shit. I sat at the table, waiting for the others to make their appearance. I sure as hell wasn't going to go see Lucy alone, but I wasn't sure if I wanted Tabby to go or not. Not after what happened last night. I rubbed my jaw where Tabby had punched me. It hurt.

Tabby wandered in and plunked down next to me. "Done sulking yet?"

"No, I'll have you know, I'm not done sulking yet." I crossed my arms.

She rolled her eyes at me. "My God, you are such a big baby. Wanna grow up a little so we can get things done here?"

I picked up my shirt, revealing the bruises that had appeared overnight.

She stared at my body. "Damn."

"Yeah, and your soul swallower threw me when I prayed at him."

"What made it stop?" she asked.

I smiled. "I cussed at it."

Her features twisted, as if she couldn't decide if she was amused or confused. "What?"

I nodded. "Yup, I cussed at it."

"That doesn't make any sense. You don't make any sense, Jimmy. No sense at all."

"I know," I said. "But if I made sense, I wouldn't be as interesting."

"True, very true." She wiped her hands on her jeans. "So, what are we doing?"

"We get the proof we need for Lucy's exorcism like before," I said. "That's my priority." I thought about it for a moment. "Maybe you and I will start sleeping in shifts."

She grabbed my hand and turned it palm up, looking at the various bruises that dotted me. "God, I'm sorry, Jimmy. I didn't realize it was this bad. I kind of hoped you were kidding, or it was a dream. Are you okay?"

I nodded. "Yeah, just bruised. The biggest problem is that we don't know enough about this thing messing with Lucy. I don't know if it's leaving Lucy at times to cause havoc or if it is bringing other things in."

"If it's bringing other things in, how do we stop it?" Tabby asked. "I mean, I warded that room upstairs."

Everything else was nuts about this place, maybe someone or something had damaged Tabby's spellwork. "Maybe we should check upstairs to make sure."

Something had happened. The black figure should not have gotten in. I doubted if a shadow person was what was attacking Lucy, but there was so much about paranormal junk I didn't know.

As soon as Tabby and I opened the door to the attic, we could smell something foul. Gone was the lackadaisical tour; we headed straight for the attic room. The symbols Tabby had made with the chalk were burnt black and looked as if a great claw had scratched through each one. The door to the attic room lay wide open.

Tabby snorted. "Guess we know how it's getting in."

"So what do we do?" I asked.

She shrugged. "I guess we'll leave this room alone. I don't have anything else."

"Nothing?"

She shook her head. "Nope."

I blinked. "You're serious."

"Completely. If I knew of anything else to do, I would come out with it. It's not like I can make things the way we want them."

"All right, let's figure out then how the hell to help Lucy." I wiped the back of my neck with my hand. "Jesus Christ."

Never in a million years did I ever think I would be dealing with something like this. I wanted to say that it felt like it was too hard, that I wanted to give up, but that wasn't true. Maybe Lucy would speak to me if I made her mad. I needed her speaking something other than Russian. The church could find a reason to reject the Russian. If I could get Lucy speaking Latin or Greek, now that would be real proof.

"Before we start, I want you to hide this from me." I turned to Tabby, taking a breath, and handing her my phone.

"Why?" She took the phone from me, staring at it.

"I have an idea. Just do it, please." I counted my breaths as she left, calming my heart and steadying my nerves. When she returned a few minutes later, I asked, "You didn't eat anything, did you?"

"No, what's up?"

I exhaled, slowly. "Because, before something like this, it's best to fast—like you do with your witchy stuff."

"Why?"

"Demons do gross things. I don't want to go into detail, but they do things that will make it hard not to vomit if they so choose. I think also there's something about fasting that helps you keep your head clear."

She raised an eyebrow.

"I know. It sounds like a bunch of bullshit. I know your stuff has reasons for fasting. I imagine they're somewhat similar. I'm trying to get used to it all. If it helps, I never thought I would have to fend off a soul sucker."

She paused, thinking. "What about our strength if this takes a long time?"

"If what takes a long time? All we're doing is talking to Lucy today," I said.

We made our way to Lucy's room. When we got to the hallway, I stopped. "If we do end up doing an exorcism, I can guarantee it will take a long time. But you can take breaks. Usually, an exorcism session only lasts a couple of hours."

"How do you know that?" she asked.

"The internet."

"Boy, are we in trouble." Tabby stepped back and let me knock on Lucy's door.

I took a deep breath.

"Lucy?" I said as I opened the door and entered the room. It was still full of that foul odor. At the doorway, the room felt normal, but closer to Lucy's bed, it was so cold I could see my breath. "Good morning, Lucy."

Lucy glanced at Tabby and cocked her head to the side. "Who's the cunt?"

I nodded toward Tabby. "Just a friend. We'd like to ask you some questions."

Lucy let forth a strange gurgling growl.

"What is your name?" I asked Lucy.

She rolled her bloody eyes. "It is whatever you think it is."

I could tread no further with that type of question. To do so would be doing an exorcism on our own, and I wasn't going there.

"How are you feeling today?" Tabby asked.

"Ahh," Lucy said. "What a kind bitch. I'm doing well, dearie. Did you like your present?"

"What present?" Tabby asked.

Lucy grinned, revealing her broken teeth.

"Your visitor." Lucy let forth that broken laugh.

"Now Lucy, I have a question," I said.

"And what is that, Priest?"

"I've misplaced my cell phone, do you know where it is?" I asked.

"And why should I help you?" she snarled.

"It's up to you," I said. "I thought I would ask in case you knew."

Lucy smiled again then focused her eyes on Tabby. "Why don't you ask her, she's the one you told to hide it from you."

And there it was, at last, proof. "Please, Lucy. Think of it like a game."

Lucy's eyes rolled back in her head and she farted so long I thought she would hurt something. The smell that issued forth fouled the air so much my eyes watered and the back of my throat burned.

"A game, eh? Well, maybe you should check the kitchen.

Victoria's pantry under the dried pasta."

We left her then and there. I closed the door behind me. Tabby handed me her phone and I turned on the video feature so we could have documentation of our finding the lost object. My hands shook. I took a deep breath and steadied myself. A shaky cam video wasn't going to do anyone any good.

As we got to the stairs, Tabby stopped. "Why does Tor like the kitchen so much?"

I shrugged. It didn't take a rocket scientist to see Tor used food like other people would use drugs—to cope.

Tabby sighed. "No really? Black died in the kitchen. Will told her that when he told you the story, right?"

She did have a point. There was no weird feeling in the kitchen minus the heaviness that always pervaded the home at Lucy's presence. "Probably before that. She didn't seem shocked when Will told me the story."

"Then why doesn't the kitchen scare the shit out of her?" Tabby asked.

"Maybe because it doesn't feel spooky. I don't know."

"She seems to react easily to everything else, it seems strange." Tabby leaned back.

I really didn't know what to say. Tor's penchant for the dramatic had irritated me more than once. Knowing she was hanging out in a room where someone died should have had some sort of effect.

When we reached the kitchen, Tor and Will looked at us oddly. I suppose we did look weird: me leading, holding the phone in front of me, and Tabby bringing up the rear.

I opened the door to the pantry and turned on the light. Like everything else to do with the kitchen, it was arranged immaculately, except for the bags of pasta. I held the phone forward and moved the bags aside. There was my phone all right, but dented and with a busted screen.

I picked it up and pressed the power button. Nothing happened.

"I didn't do that, Jimmy," Tabby said.

"I know."

I stopped the recording on Tabby's phone and handed it to her. Then, I set my ruined phone on the table.

"Lucy did this." I pointed to the cracked screen.

Will glanced up at me as if he were looking over the top of a pair of glasses, even though he wasn't wearing any. Then, he shook himself. "Wait what?"

I nodded. "Somehow, she did it. One of the things I need to prove for someone being possessed is that they know the location of lost objects so I had Tabby hide my phone from me. How, I don't know, but Lucy knew Tabby hid it, and somehow she broke it."

"Well, Jimmy," Tor swallowed hard, "we'll get you another phone."

"It's insured. It's just strange. It didn't have to break it." The corner of my mouth crept into a smirk. "I guess there is no doubt, this thing really doesn't like me."

Tabby chuckled. "Of course not, Jimmy. You were a priest. There isn't anything in that book of yours that says you have to be an active priest to perform an exorcism, is there?"

"No, but the exorcist is supposed to be approved by the bishop, so I hardly think a bishop would grant permission for a defrocked priest to perform an exorcism."

"Well then," Tabby said, waving her arms with a flourish. "No matter what, you are a threat, Jimmy Holiday. You could possibly cast it out."

Both Will and Tor became excited then. They sat higher in their seats, their legs shaking and their eyes sparkling with energy.

"Then there's no reason to wait for the church," Tor said.

I held up my hands. "Oh, hell no. We are not doing that. You forget, I know about as much about this as you do. We are getting the church involved."

"Why?" Tabby stared at me, eyes flashing.

I held up my hand. "No, Tabby. Don't get riled. I mean, what do you know about exorcism?"

"Not much."

"That means you know as much as I do, or almost. You've seen the movies. All I have on you is this one little book."

She snorted. "Well, if the word of God is only a book, the Salem witches should never have had a thing to worry about then."

"Let's not talk about it anymore. I'm hungry. I'm tired, and I want to go get a new phone."

Tor jumped up from her chair and pulled a package of Danish out of the pantry.

"Did you get what you needed from Lucy this morning?" Will asked.

I nodded. "One part of it. There are still three more things on the list, but it's a step forward."

Will nodded. "Yeah, it is."

#

After we finished eating, Will followed me into the library to get rid of the broken chair. The pieces had ended up near the fireplace. The legs snapped from the base in pointed, splintered ends. I rubbed my ribs.

"What other things do you need to prove?" he asked, eyeing the chair.

"I'd rather not say," I said. "Honestly, that way if I'm asked if Lucy could have been influenced, then I can say without a doubt that there is no way she could have been coached."

"But, don't you trust me?" His eyes looked wounded—

round and a little too wide.

I ran my hands through my hair. "Will, it's not about trust. It isn't. Everything with the church is about perception. What they will look at is not only if Lucy's possessed, but if it gets out, how it will look in terms of the perception of the church."

"I thought the church was about helping people," Will said.

I chuckled. "Oh they are, but they are about politics too. I should know."

Will said nothing more. He and I took the broken pieces of the chair into the basement and stacked them next to that week's garbage.

I stood up straight and stretched my back. Then, I noticed something unusual. For the most part, "haunted houses" are creepiest in the basement. Here, the basement was quiet and warm. It didn't feel threatening at all. The one weird thing was on the far wall. A couple of metal rings attached to the concrete with brackets. In the back of my mind, I remembered the crack of a whip. Black and his wife. It happened here. But still, the basement felt safe somehow. I couldn't explain it.

I kept my thoughts to myself. I already had Will jumping from one conclusion to the next. It was hard to tell how he would feel if he knew what I was thinking.

We left the basement and headed to the kitchen.

"Jimmy," Tor said. "I *am* going to get you a new phone. My daughter broke it, it's only right."

"Tor, honestly, it's okay. I already told you, I have insurance."

Will came up from behind me and patted Tor on the shoulder. He turned toward me. "You might as well give it up, Jimmy. When Tor sets her mind to something, that's it."

Tor grinned. She ambled over to the sink, put her hands in the soapy water and began to wash dishes. "Will is going to take you wherever you need to go to get a new phone."

"Are the two of you going to be okay while we're gone?" I asked.

Tabby laughed. "We'll be fine. Tor and I already decided we won't leave each other alone the rest of the day. There's too much that's strange here. Plus, this is bath day for Lucy, and I'm sure Tor could use some help."

I nodded. "Be careful."

#

Will ushered me into the 4Runner soon after. Some things didn't add up about Will and Tor. The car was a prime example. Why did they have a mansion, but an old car? It made no sense at all.

Will pulled the car out of the driveway as we headed for the main road. "We got about an hour drive."

"Is everything an hour from here?" I asked.

Will laughed. "No, there's a Wal-Mart about a half an hour away. Not much else, but at least there's a Wal-Mart."

"Do you think you would have liked living in Sorrow's Point if this hadn't happened to Lucy?"

Will inclined his head in thought as he drove. "I think so. It was out of the way, away from danger, or so we believed. It seemed like a decent town to raise a kid in, ya know? We haven't been able to do most of what we planned."

"What do you mean?" I asked. There it was again. The denial. He'd either forgotten or pushed out of his mind what small town living had been like for us.

"In D.C., we took the metro most places. We used the car rarely. Here, we need a car all the time." He scratched his hand. "We were going to get a new car after we moved, but I haven't bothered. Lucy takes up so much time."

All his hopes had dried with Lucy's illness. He was broken—a shell of the man he once was.

"When Lucy gets better, are you going to sell the house?"

Will sighed. "No way we can. This house had been on the market for over ten years."

"Isn't there something about nondisclosure of a murder? You might be able to get out of it… probably," I said.

"If we'd known, it likely wouldn't have mattered. Tor still would have wanted the house. Hell, the Black family paid for a caretaker to keep up the grounds and make any repairs as needed. No way we could afford that. If we sell the house, it would probably take forever. So we'll be staying there."

Not what I wanted to hear. "Will, if that thing got Lucy to let it out once, what's to say it won't happen again?"

Will grasped the steering wheel so tight his knuckles turned white. "I don't know what to do, Jimmy. If Tor and I give up the house, we'll have to go live with Tor's mother. Mom and Dad died one right after the other not long after we moved into this house. Asking Mom about Lucy was one of the last conversations I had with her. There literally isn't anywhere else for us to go."

"You could stay with me." It flew out of my mouth before I could stop it. I couldn't imagine what that would be like. A nightmare most likely.

"That's really nice, Jimmy, but I couldn't do that to you." Will moaned. "Besides, I can't see Tor surviving in that kitchen of yours."

I laughed. "Yeah, somehow I don't think she'd find my retro fridge groovy."

Will smiled sadly. "You know something?"

"What?"

"Lucy would love it."

Chapter Twenty-One

Development

"TABBY, WANT TO help me give Lucy a bath?" Tor asked.

I looked up from the eBook I was reading on my phone. "Sure. I can do that."

Jimmy and Will had been gone for a while. And I had no qualms about making myself useful. Better that than sitting around.

I followed Tor up to Lucy's room. The stench wasn't as strong as the last time I'd been up there, but it still smelled pretty bad. Almost like the pee smell in nursing homes. My nose wrinkled.

"Lucy, time for your bath," Tor said, opening the door.

I followed behind. Lucy sat in her bed quietly. Tor walked out of the room and through another door.

Lucy smirked at me. The child-like part of me wanted to stick my tongue out at her, but I didn't. This was a possessed kid. Who knew what she would do?

When Tor came back in, Lucy let her undo the bindings. Tor picked her up and carried her into the adjoining bathroom.

"Could you get some towels?" Tor asked me.

I followed them both and grabbed some from the shelf in the bathroom. Then I set them on top of the toilet while Tor set Lucy into the bathtub.

"Water okay?" Tor asked Lucy.

She nodded.

I let my eyes wander while Tor bathed Lucy. Leaning against the wall, I poised, ready in case Tor needed anything. But so far, she had everything under control.

My eyes closed, just for a moment, and Tor screamed.

My lids jerked open and my gaze flew in the direction of the bath. A woman's razor arched through the air and landed on Tor's arm for what had to be the second go. It slid down, cutting her skin to ribbons.

Lucy laughed in a choppy growl like it was the funniest thing she had ever seen.

"Oh. My. God."

Lucy's gazed landed on me as sharp as the blade. The razor rose up from Tor's arm and started for me. My knees wanted to go weak, but I focused and grounded my energy.

"Hail, Guardians of the Watchtower! Protect us from evil. Protect us from this servant of darkness!" I put my essence into the words, but Lucy only laughed. The razor dropped to the floor.

I clutched a towel from the stack, wrapped it tightly around Tor's arm, and dragged her out of the room.

"We need to get you some help," I said.

"I'll be okay. We can't leave Lucy."

My thoughts spun, but I couldn't argue with her. The child—possessed or not— couldn't be left alone. "Shit."

#

Finally, back in Sorrow's Point, my phone had been replaced with something far fancier. I didn't bother trying to stop Will. He seemed to want to do something to make it all up to me. I still felt guilty though. If they were having financial problems, I didn't want to add to it, and a fancy phone was an expenditure that didn't make sense.

We left the car in the front drive, walked up the huge stone steps and entered through the door. Will paused for a moment in front of me. I heard nothing. He stepped forward and I followed as he headed toward the kitchen. It was a hell of a sight. Bloody rags covered the table. Tabby held a towel to Tor's arm.

"What the hell happened?" I asked.

"Tor was giving Lucy a bath in the tub. She seemed so complacent. Tor thought it would be okay. It was…until Lucy used the razor," Tabby said.

"Shit," Will said. "Are you okay, Tor?"

She nodded. "I think I need stitches."

"I'll take her to the hospital," Tabby said, "you two check on Lucy."

I searched the room. "And where's Lucy?"

Tabby stared at me, her eyes wide. "She's still in the bathtub."

Will and I ran out of the kitchen toward the staircase and dashed upstairs. He darted into Lucy's bedroom with me following close at his heels. Bits of blood coated the bathroom; some spattered on the wall, while the rest sprayed the bathtub and Lucy. Where the blood dots hadn't landed, the blood smeared as if Lucy had been rubbing it on her body. She sat in the tub, playing with toys as if nothing was going on.

Will snatched Lucy out of the tub while I held the door open. After Will got Lucy dressed and into bed, we strapped her in. I ran back into the bathroom and rummaged through cupboards until I found a clean wash cloth. I wetted it in the sink and walked back into Lucy's room. I handed it to Will. He managed to get most of the blood off Lucy.

We left her alone and went back into the bathroom and cleaned up the blood.

"Where did Lucy get the razor?" I asked after Will had closed the door to Lucy's room and we headed downstairs.

He stopped in the middle of the staircase. "I don't know. There shouldn't have been a razor in her room. Tor shaves in our bathroom."

I wobbled a little where I was perched above Will on the stairs. "That's strange."

Will nodded. "She has to be getting out of the restraints somehow. So far, she hasn't left her bed on camera."

"Does Lucy know where Tor keeps her razors?" I asked.

"Probably," Will said. "Lucy used to beg to take a bath with her mommy."

I nodded. "She could be telekinetic."

Will stopped at the bottom of the stairs. "What?"

"You know, telekinesis. It's the ability to move objects with your mind. If she isn't getting out of bed, she's bringing things to her, or using something else or someone else to get what she wants."

"How?"

I sighed. "Tabby said your house is built near a ley line—a direct power source that magical entities can use as a doorway to other worlds. This house, especially that room upstairs, is kind of a conduit for that line. I think Lucy is using the house to bring things in to help her."

"Could this line be where this thing came from to begin with?"

I shrugged. "It's possible. I think old man Black messed with a lot of things he shouldn't have. I believe he got himself possessed, and ate his family. Then, this thing kept causing problems, so the town stepped in and brought in the experts to bind it to that mirror. Apparently, it wasn't bound enough because it could still speak to Lucy, and got her to let it out."

"How do you know that?" Will asked.

"I don't. It's my current hypothesis. We should know for sure after the exorcism."

#

Three hours later, Tabby and Tor shuffled into the house. An ace bandage covered Tor's arm with a support board strapped to it.

"What'd they say?" I asked.

Tor sat in the chair opposite from me. "They gave me a tetanus shot, and I have to go back in two weeks to get the stitches out. Thank God it was a disposable razor. It didn't cut too deep, but bled a lot. And it hurts like hell." She smiled sadly. "Guess I won't be cooking for a while."

I patted Tor on the shoulder. "It's okay. We'll survive. Tabby can cook, and so can I. Get some rest. Will and I'll head to the grocery store."

Will dropped me off at the market while he went to the pharmacy to get Tor's prescription filled. As I wandered the aisles, my thoughts drifted back to Tor and the attack.

Was the demon putting a spell over Will and Tor? The constant attacks had to be doing more to them than what they were showing me. One minute, Tor was all upset and squealing at the thought of something Lucy had done. The next, after she'd been directly attacked, she seemed almost passive. Will alternated between being irritated at Tor and pushing toward exorcism to sitting around and doing nothing. None of it made sense except the demon. It had to be affecting their psyche.

I hopped into the car as soon as Will pulled up in front of the market. It was weird. His face was a blank mask. He was so nonchalant about it all, not concerned about Tor; of course, maybe I was looking too far into it. Maybe that's how it is when you fall out of love with someone. I didn't know a thing about that.

"Are you afraid to die?" Will asked me as we left the parking lot.

I peered at him out of the corner of my eye. "Not really, no."

"Why not?" Will asked. "What if this is all there is? What if the only thing left is nothing?"

I laughed a little. He must be in denial. There was no other excuse for it. "Will, your daughter is possessed, right?"

"Yes."

"Then you're contradicting yourself. How can you believe there is nothing out there after we die if you're afraid of demons?" I paused for a moment to let it all sink in. "There's a line from an old movie that puts it as plain as I could ever say it, 'If you are afraid of dying, you will see devils trying to take your life away, but if you have made your peace, the devils are really angels, taking you to heaven.'"

"What movie is that from?" he asked.

"*Jacob's Ladder.*"

"Isn't that a scary movie? I mean, you were all priestly when that came out. Was that allowed?" Will asked.

I rolled my eyes. "There's nothing out there that says a priest can't watch a scary movie. Is it looked down on if you watch *Harry Potter*? Yes, but you aren't punished for it. *The Exorcist* is a little different though. It's banned by the church."

"Aren't the *Harry Potter* books banned too?" he asked.

I chuckled. "No. The pope at the time declared them evil, but they aren't banned."

"Tell me, how does that make sense?"

I snickered. "It doesn't."

Why he chose to bring all that up, I had no idea, but then, I reminded myself that I knew little of his religious upbringing.

"How long do you think Lucy's exorcism will take?" he asked.

I turned toward him. He seemed shakier than usual. "I don't know. It depends on how powerful the demon is."

Will wiped his mouth with his hand. He was so nervous he was sweating. "Can... can the sins of a parent cause a child to be possessed?"

So that was it? He'd done something and was afraid what he'd done had caused Lucy's possession? His whole demeanor was caused by simple guilt. It would be a good idea to keep all that in mind.

"It depends on the sin, Will," I said. "If you'd say, hurt someone or beat them up, then no, you couldn't have caused Lucy's possession."

Will swallowed.

I reached over and decreased the heat in the car.

"What is an example of a parent's sin that could cause the possession of a child?" he asked.

I took a deep breath. "About the only thing would be if you participated in a black mass and promised her soul to the devil."

"Jesus Christ, do people do that?"

I nodded. "Very evil people, yes."

Will sighed. His knuckles gripped tighter on the dashboard. "What about adultery?"

There it was, the admission I'd been waiting for. It accounted for Will's attitude, it accounted for the tension between Will and Tor. What it didn't account for was anything to do with Lucy. At least, it had nothing to do with Lucy being possessed.

I rubbed my chin with my fingers. "No, adultery doesn't cause a child to be possessed. Adultery will cause you to spend some years in purgatory to atone for your sins, but it doesn't cause demonic possession."

I thought about it. If Lucy were older, it could be conceivably possible Lucy could try to make believe something was wrong to get back at her parents for their problems, but possession was something that didn't make a lot of sense in that scenario. Especially with all the supernatural shit going on with Lucy.

When it came down to it, what I felt didn't matter all that much.

"So, anything I did, didn't cause Lucy to be like this?" Will asked.

"Not to my knowledge. The way I see it is you stumbled on a house Tor felt drawn to, possibly because it's so damn huge. Unfortunately, this house had a hidden past your real estate agent should have told you about before you bought it. Then, something drew Lucy to the mirror. Even Tor admitted that." I glanced at Will. He was nodding. "I figure Lucy wanted to know if the glass was black all the way through, or if it was covered up, so she inadvertently released the thing, whatever it is and wherever it originally came from."

Tears began to well up in Will's eyes. "I love my little girl, Jimmy. I don't want her to die."

"I know, Will. I know."

We pulled into the driveway of the house. I felt drained, but I thought it was worth it. Will had gotten something huge off his chest. Honestly, he could use some therapy, and I'm sure Tor needed the same. Lucy needed a lot of things. I wished I could give her the help she needed.

We stopped and unloaded everything from the car. Will paused and stared up at the sky.

"Looks like it might snow," he said.

"Maybe."

#

After dinner, Tabby and I washed dishes and Tor directed us where and how to put things away. I would like to have said it was because we were trusted, but I really think it's because Tor felt so bad. Her face blanched white and the corners of her mouth pursed.

"I think I'm going to go to bed," Tor said.

Tabby turned from the sink. "Are you all right?"

Tor nodded. "Just hurting. I think I want to lie down for a while. Get all that stuff as best you can. I don't care anymore."

We watched her go in silence.

"That's not good," Tabby said.

"No, it's not, and after what I learned this afternoon, I'm not surprised."

"Can you tell me about it?" she asked.

I shook my head. "It was never specified for me not to tell anyone else, but the subject matter alone makes it something I'd rather not talk about."

Tabby nodded. "I think I can figure it out."

"This is a very unhappy family."

"Yeah. Too unhappy."

I found Will in the living room soon after. He was sitting alone, staring off into space. I knocked on the door jamb, Tabby close at my heels. "Mind if we come in?"

Will looked up. "Sure."

Tabby and I sat on the sofa. Will was nursing a beer. I could see the condensation dripping off the can and onto the coaster.

"Tor went to bed," Tabby said.

I rubbed my hand across the pile on the fabric of the sofa. "She said she was hurting, so she was going to go lay down."

"I still can't believe Lucy did that to her," he said.

I believed Lucy did it. She'd almost knocked me off the ladder, brought in a soul sucker to come after Tabby, and I got hurt by the same creature. I had no trouble believing Lucy was capable of anything.

Will's eyes narrowed. He must have figured my thoughts by

his expression.

"It's not that I don't believe she actually did it," he said. "It's that I find it hard to believe this is the same Lucy I've known for six years."

"That's the point, Will. Demons like to change the most beautiful things into the most profane. I suppose, in a way, they do these things because they aren't worthy of God's love. If they make us like them, maybe they think God will no longer love us."

Tabby's eyebrows furrowed. "Is it really so simple?"

I shrugged. "Probably not, but it's how I've always understood it. I might be right, but my theories don't mean much at all."

"And if you're wrong?" Will asked.

I took a breath. "Then I'm wrong. I wasn't made perfect, and God doesn't expect us to be perfect. Otherwise, there would be no reason for purgatory."

"You should be a theologist," Tabby said.

I scratched my arm. "It wouldn't be the life for me. I like to help people. If I were a theologian, I would spend most of my time studying the word of God. I did that in seminary. God and I have a certain understanding. I believe in Him. I love Him, and I generally try to be a good person."

"And what does God get?" Tabby asked.

I grinned. I couldn't help it. I didn't know what she was asking for, but I answered her as truthfully as I could. "He gets amused."

#

Oddly enough, I woke refreshed the next morning, even though I'd not had a lot of sleep. Tabby agreed to try to ward the room today, so we wouldn't have to sleep in shifts again. Yet even with the off and on two hour spurts I felt better than I had in a while. Maybe it was having a plan, or maybe it was I was so damn tired. Either way, I knew it would be best to work with Lucy well rested and energetic.

"Sleep okay?" I asked as Tabby returned from her shower.

She put her stuff in her bag. "It was quiet. Almost too quiet, if you know what I mean. I can't help but wonder if this is the calm before something worse happens."

I nodded. "Do you need anything for your ward thingy?"

Tabby chuffed me on the arm. "I haven't even had a chance to look, Mr. Smartypants. You're lucky I know you so well, otherwise I would have no idea what the hell you're talking about." She motioned with her hand toward the library door. "Go get your bath. We'll tackle this after."

"Yes, Ma'am."

When I came into the library after my bath, I saw one hell of a mess. "Um, what's this?" I motioned toward the herbs scattered all over the floor. They were sort of arranged in piles. One appeared to be basil, but there was a pile of brown stuff with stems too, a pile of slightly brownish purple stuff, and a lot of piles of green powder.

Tabby grinned. "I'm in luck. Tor had enough for me to do this."

"Did you ask her if you could use them?" I said with a raised eyebrow.

She looked like she wanted to hurt me—bad. "Yes, you idiot. I didn't come out of a cave you know."

"How long is this going to take?"

"As long as it takes. Right now. I'm organizing and figuring this out."

I nodded.

"Why don't you go in the kitchen with Tor? I know you haven't had breakfast, and you'll give Tor something to do."

"Have you had breakfast?" I asked.

"I wanted to fast before I did this. Now go!" She stood up and pushed me toward the door.

Not wanting to irritate her any further, I went. I didn't like leaving Tabby alone, but she hadn't given me a choice. I wanted to help her, I really did, but I guess my questions and reactions were more irritating than helpful.

I wandered into the kitchen. Tor was sitting at the table looking completely dejected. "You okay?"

She looked up. "Will and I had a fight. He left about two hours ago."

I sat across from her at the table. "Need to talk about it?"

"Will confessed," Tor scratched her good arm, "about his affair. Somehow he expected me to give in, to tell him it was all right. Goddamn it, it isn't all right."

"Can you forgive him?" I asked.

"Right now, I can tell you I don't want to. Do I need to? Probably, but I feel betrayed."

"Well, if you went by the church, they don't believe in divorce, but some things about the church need updating. I'm not saying you should divorce Will, I'm saying you should explore every option."

She stared at me. "What would you do?"

"Honestly?"

She nodded.

Given what I'd seen my parents go through, staying together for the kids alone didn't work. In fact, it turned everybody miserable. Granted, neither Tor nor Will were alcoholics, but it would still be a disaster. Lucy would grow up in a home that appeared normal, but was anything but. I'd been there. I lived it. It sucked.

"I can't say I would definitely do this because what we think we'll do and what we end up doing are usually nothing alike. I think I couldn't stand that betrayal. I would get out as soon as I could."

"Even if you had kids?" she asked.

"Especially then. I lived in a house where my parents didn't love each other. Each year got worse instead of better. If I didn't have the church to escape to, I would probably, at the very least, be a drug addict. Most likely, I'd be dead by now."

"Hmm....I have a lot to think about," she said, wiping at her eyes. She cast a sad smile. "Want some breakfast? My arm isn't hurting as badly as I thought it would."

I smiled. "Whatever you want to make."

#

After breakfast, Tor went outside. I crept back near the library. Tabby was drawing symbols in the air and stirring a mixture in a small iron pot. I didn't have any idea what she was doing, but it was interesting.

I heard a noise, something with great claws scrambling up the wooden steps to the upper level. I turned my head, but of course there was nothing there. Out of the corner of my eye, I managed to catch a flash of green where Tabby was working. For a small moment, the green that appeared shifted into a symbol. As I looked toward Tabby, I saw nothing but her drawing in the air. This time, I could tell what she was drawing was, in fact, the symbol I had seen.

I allowed Tabby to believe as she believed, but there was a strong part of me that didn't take it seriously. For whatever reason, and maybe it was my church training, it was hard for me to believe in magic unless it had to do with black magic. Technically, you could call transubstantiation a type of magic ritual, but the church didn't view it that way. Doing so would get you branded a heretic. Then again, I was already considered something less than dirt by the church. It couldn't get much worse.

But with Tabby, I always knew she was anything but. She was a good egg, and I believed, without a doubt, she would never do anything evil to another living soul. That knowledge still didn't erase the fact that I now knew Tabby's witchy stuff was real. It turned my stomach sour, but there was also something comforting about being able to see it. In *knowing* it was there. Her power didn't need faith for it to work. What I thought was blasphemy, wasn't it?

I turned my head to the side again. This time more than one symbol appeared. Each had its own color: mostly reds, oranges, blues, greens and yellows. Beautiful to look at, but not something I'd seen before. I wondered if it was only Tabby's magic I could see, or if something had changed within me.

As soon as Tabby finished, she glanced up and noticed me. She blushed. "How long were you standing there?"

I grinned. "You would probably say too long, but it was long enough for me."

"Long enough for what?"

"For me to figure things out."

Chapter Twenty-Two

Cocoon

AFTER EVERYTHING WAS put to rights in the library and the herbs were swept up from the floor, I said, "Tor's had a bad morning."

Tabby furrowed her brow and wiped the sweat from her upper lip. "What do you mean?"

"Remember how I told you things were bad yesterday?"

Tabby set her bag on the sofa.

"Well," I said, "Will fessed up to Tor. We're either already in the middle of World War III or waiting for it to start."

Tabby tapped her chin with her fingers. "Do you think that's why things were calm last night?"

"I dunno."

Tabby brushed her hair off her forehead. "So what's on the agenda?"

"Today, we see if Lucy will speak to us, *really* speak to us."

Tabby waved a hand toward the door. "Lead the way."

I grabbed my notebook and a felt tipped marker. I hadn't forgotten what Lucy had done to her mother with a razor blade, and I wasn't about to take any chances.

After we left the library, I paused at the bottom of the stairs and took a deep breath.

"Okay," I said more to center my resolve than to Tabby,

"here we go."

I began ascending, Tabby followed. There were no sounds, just the creaking of us walking the stairs. The old wood groaned with every step. How did this house look when Black had it? Granted the furniture was Black's, but somehow I imagined the house looked darker, more sinister when he lived there. I was speculating too much again, letting the *special something* of the house distract me from the real issues. It didn't matter what the house was like when Black had it except for maybe the attic room, but the house, at this point, had nothing to do with Lucy at all. Mr. Black, however, I think had a lot to do with Lucy.

As soon as I reached the top and turned toward Lucy's wing, the laughter started. Then she began to sing, "Where oh were has my little priest gone? Where oh where can he be!"

The lights winked out of my vision. Darkness. I was blind. I heard nothing. The void intensified like I'd been transported to a space of nothingness. I was alone. I'd completely disappeared.

Demon tricks are many, I thought. *It wants fear. You need to relax.*

Tabby's hands on my arm hit me first. I opened my eyes. Things returned to normal.

"Jimmy?" she asked. "Are you okay?"

Her fingers squeezed. I smiled at her, but inside spiders crawled under my skin. "Yep."

"What happened?"

"Lucy playing a trick." I reached for the wall to orient my body to the surroundings. "Nothing more."

Tabby's eyes darkened and she stared at me for what seemed like forever. "Are you sure?"

I nodded. "Come on. I think Lucy's a bit bored."

"Are you sure this is a good idea?" she asked, trying to keep up with me as I started down the hallway.

"It doesn't matter if it's good or not," I said. "It's the only option we have."

Tabby ran in front of me and stopped, putting her hands on her hips. "What are you blathering about? There are always options."

I shook my head. "Not for Lucy there aren't. Time's running out, Tabby. You've seen her. She isn't well. I don't know if the possession is causing her health to fail, but I know this little girl is dying. There isn't time for me to be chicken shit."

She paused then nodded grimly.

"All right," I said. "Let's go."

When we got to Lucy's door, it was so cold I could see the puffs of my breath. "She's getting stronger."

Tabby stared into my eyes, a wild look in the depths of her pupils. Hell, I was scared. Lucy was something I hadn't faced before. She was creepy as sin, and I think she knew it. She seemed to get a charge by making people feel uncomfortable, not like a six-year-old at all. She once was a normal kid, and now she wasn't.

I reached toward the door, but as soon as I touched the knob, I jerked my hand away.

"What's wrong?" Tabby asked.

"It's cold. Ice cold." I used the hem of my shirt and opened it.

Lucy was in her bed, grinning like a Cheshire cat. "So you've come to visit me, Priest?"

"Yes, Lucy," I said. "Tabby and I thought that we would sit with you for a while and visit. I'm sure you're bored."

Lucy chuckled like a woodpecker hammering at a tree. "Oh, I find things to keep me entertained. A little chaos here, a little thanatos there."

Thanatos, classical Greek for death. No way at all Lucy could have learned about it.

"What is it about thanatos you like, Lucy?" I wanted to

show that she understood. I could only hope she'd comply.

Lucy fixed those ugly, bloody eyes on me. "Thanatos, dear Father Holiday, is the point to everything. Through thanatos, I get what I want, and each time I experience death, I get to go after another soul. Through that I am reborn."

I nodded. "Does thanatos liberate you?"

It cackled. "Liberaté me. Liberaté me!"

My brain flashed back to the note I received during my dream. Shame I couldn't have used that before. Okay, we had Greek and Latin, what was next?

"Du bist interessant, Vater Holiday," Lucy said.

I paused. Holy crap, now she was speaking German. This was proof. No doubt.

"Thank you, Lucy," I said.

"Nechevo," she answered.

Good God. Greek, Latin, German, and Russian in the space of five minutes. It would be difficult for the church to deny this.

I tapped my fingers on the footboard of Lucy's bed. "We'll go now, Lucy," I said. "You need your rest."

She smiled.

Tabby and I left the room as nonchalantly as possible. I was glad we kept our cool. Never a good idea to give the demon any emotional ammo. I waited until we were downstairs in the kitchen before I exploded. "I can't believe it!"

"Shh," Tabby held her finger in front of my mouth.

"Shit, sorry. I never expected that. Four languages she has no way of knowing. I feel so damn…I don't know…lucky."

Tabby stared at me, her eyes haunted and far away. "Why should you feel lucky?"

I must have sounded like a cross between a madman and an idiot. "I meant I can't believe how this has turned out. We couldn't have better luck for Lucy. The church is going to have a hard time ignoring this evidence."

"I don't know, Jimmy," Tabby said. "Is it enough?"

It hit me then—what she meant. I was so excited by Lucy's capacity for language I was missing the point. The church, depending on their mood, would do what they liked. We had another piece of the puzzle that would make it hard for them to ignore. Hard, but not impossible.

#

That evening, Will camped out in the living room. We weren't given the full explanation about what happened, but I imagine it was going to take some time for Tor to forgive Will, if she decided to do so at all.

Tabby and I left Will alone and got ourselves arranged in the library for the night. Part of me felt like I should feel guilty for not asking Will to share the library with us, but for me, it was nice to have a break from everything.

Round about three—God I was getting tired of that number—Tabby and I woke to a loud booming noise. I jerked my head up. The doorway to the library glowed green and a huge dark figure loomed in the doorway. Every few seconds, it would raise a massive hand and strike at the open space of the doorway. He looked like a cross between a mountain troll and a Mack truck, all organic yet cybernetic. With each strike, the boom intensified.

I stared at Tabby. "What the hell is that?"

She stared at me, eyes wide. "I have no idea." Pulling the blanket back from her legs, she sat up, still staring at the doorway. "If the wards hold…"

The thing kept pounding. The symbols vibrated each time the creature beat against the wards. With every boom, I wanted to back away, but I stayed where I was. There was only so far I could go.

"Why do they glow green like that?" I asked.

Her lips pulled into a frown. "What are you talking about?"

Tabby sat on her knees, staring over the back of the couch at the thing.

"The wards, they glow green each time that thing decides to bounce a hand off them." I didn't have to turn my head now to see the wards pulsate.

She cocked her head and stared at me. "Um, Jimmy?"

"Yeah?"

"That's not normal."

I slumped back onto my sofa. "What do you mean?"

She took a deep breath. "When I drew them, *I* couldn't even see them." She moved over and pointed to the main symbol, or at least its general area. "Draw it for me."

I ripped a piece of paper from my notebook and traced it as best I could. I held it out to her when I was finished.

Tabby's mouth dropped open. "Jimmy," she said. "Could you do this before?"

I shook my head. "It started today when you were warding the doorway."

She leaned closer. "Wow."

"Wow what?"

She shook herself and then paused, thinking. "You've been given a gift of sorts." She rubbed her hands up and down her arms as if trying to get rid of a chill. "Can you see other things?"

I shrugged. "Not as far as I know of." I peered around the room. "I mean, I haven't tried."

"Just...let me know if you see other things, okay?" she asked.

I nodded and swallowed hard.

Finally, the thing stopped. Nothing he could do would let him pass Tabby's wards. Thank God. He stood there for a moment, staring at us. Then with a crack he disappeared.

Chapter Twenty-Three

Revelation

"PRIEST," IT WHISPERED in my ear.

I woke up, frantically checking the library, and saw nothing. No creatures, no demons, nothing went bump in the night. Tabby was fine, resting. The blanket pulled up to her chin. The entrance to the library looked the same, normal. Nothing there.

"Priest," the voice whispered again.

I shot up and put my elbows on my knees. Was it a trap? Lucy doing something to get me to leave the library? I focused my hearing, but there was no sound. If Lucy was in medical distress, the alarms on her equipment would be going off.

"Priest," it said again.

"What," I said sharply. I thought I heard what sounded like the giggle of a little girl, but it was faint.

"Come and play with me," the voice said.

I scowled. "No, I don't think so."

It was quiet for a moment, and then the banging on the wards began again. Tabby jumped awake.

"What is it this time?" she asked.

"Absolutely nothing," I said, and I didn't lie.

She glanced around the room. "Where's the noise coming from?"

I shrugged. "Lucy. There's nothing attacking the wards that

I can see. I'm going to guess our Lucy is a mimic."

Her face went blank. "That's kind of interesting, but scary."

I nodded. "It means we're really going to have to be on our toes. If she can impersonate a noise, you know she can mimic any one of us."

"And the library is the only safe place in the house."

I scratched my head. "You could ward other places."

Tabby's face scrunched. "We saw how well that worked when I warded the room upstairs. We're lucky the wards worked here."

I sighed. She was right. For some reason the library worked. Maybe, simply, because this was not a place in the house the badness crept in. "I don't know what else to do. If we could find out exactly what that thing wants, we'd be a step closer."

Tabby ran her hands through her hair. "You told me yourself that demons are tricky."

"Yeah, so?"

She took a frustrated breath. "Don't forget what it told you. It wants Lucy's soul, but it wants more too."

"Of course it wants more, it's a demon."

Tabby rolled her eyes at me. "It's more than that, Jimmy. It's like she's affecting your brain somehow. You aren't usually this easy to jump to conclusions, and this thing with you being able to see magic…it's scary."

I stared at her. "What are we going to do about it?"

"I'm fine," she said. "You need to keep yourself in check. I don't know what's going on, but honestly, I don't like it."

I threw my hands in the air. "Dammit, Tabby, what do I need to do, huh? You know all this weird shit. I know about graphic design, saying Mass, and keeping my house from falling apart."

"Shh," Tabby put her finger over her mouth.

"Oh come on, if they didn't wake up with all the booming, I

hardly think my voice is going to wake them."

"Jimmy, God you can be such an ass. Did you notice how tired Tor was? Maybe she hears the noises, and then can't sleep. I don't know, but I think Will and Tor hear it. Maybe subconsciously, they're glad it has new people to pick on, even if they're still getting hurt."

I couldn't deny that. It had been stronger here from the beginning. Maybe I'd been dead wrong about the whole thing.

"Okay, what can I do to keep my head straight?"

Tabby grinned. "I'll go out tomorrow and get you a piece of jewelry to wear. Then I'll spell it for clarity, so that anytime you wear it, which will be all the time, it will keep your brain from getting muddled."

"Okay."

"Now, can we go back to sleep, please?" she asked.

#

After breakfast the next morning, Tabby left to get something so she could make the clarity charm for me. Will was out doing yard work, trying desperately to get Tor's approval. I offered to help, but Will gave me that look that said, "I need to do this alone, otherwise it won't matter."

Tor came in not long after Will left the house. Her arm was still wrapped, but she seemed to be in less pain than the day before.

She sat at the table beside me and stared out the window. "Tomorrow, I think I'll make bread. I could use some comfort food."

"Feeling better?" I asked.

She nodded then turned her heard toward me, staring at me in a strange way.

"Something is bothering you," she said.

"A lot of things are bothering me."

Wrapping her hands around her coffee cup, she said, "Like what?"

I settled back into my chair. This looked like it was going to take a while. "Was Lucy baptized?"

She glanced into her coffee. "Yes, at my family's church. I have the pictures somewhere. She wore my great-grandmother's christening gown."

I smiled. At least I now had another question answered. "Before you left D.C., did Lucy act upset?"

Tor stared out the window. "Not strange exactly, but alternating between clingy and withdrawn. One minute, she'd be crawling all over me or Will, the next she wanted to be left alone."

I had to tread carefully here. This was already a family in crisis. Things were bad enough without my interfering, but I needed the answers. Lucy's life might depend on something that Tor or Will would view insignificant.

I took a deep breath. "Any chance Lucy could have known about Will?"

At first, she seemed puzzled. Then her eyes darkened as she realized what I was asking. "It's possible, but I don't know how she could have."

"I guess we'll have to ask Will then," I said.

Tor snorted. "Asking Will about anything is pointless, haven't you figured that out yet?" She pushed her coffee cup away. "Now, I have a question for you. Will told me that he'd told you about the affair the day before he told me, is that true?"

I nodded. "He told me on the way back from getting my new phone. He was worried that his transgression caused Lucy's possession."

"Did it?" she asked.

"No. Plenty of kids have parents who split up and have

affairs, and most of them are never possessed. No, I don't think what Will did had anything to do with it."

She sighed. "Why Lucy then?"

I rubbed my face with my hand. "That's the question, isn't it? Is it as simple as her being the one to scratch the black paint on the mirror? Is it as simple as Lucy being a very sensitive child? I don't know. That's one of the hardest things about possession. It forces us to see what is good turned into something foul."

Tor narrowed her eyes at me. "You're very astute, you know that?"

I chuckled. "I wouldn't say that. More like for my first job, I was trained to listen, think and see how people's actions affect those around them."

"What about the molesters?" she asked.

It always came to this. The fucking perverts had forever changed the view of what was once a trusted position and I hated them for it. "Like anything else," I said. "It only takes a few bad apples to spoil the bunch. There are good priests out there. Sadly, every priest now has to fight that stigma and the molesters usually don't get enough punishment."

"What do you think should happen to them?"

The rage I felt made the acid in my stomach boil. This was going into an area I wasn't crazy to talk about. It was too close to home. "They should be killed. Molesters are broken people. Studies have been done, even castration doesn't stop them. A lot of people will argue that a molester's victims get to move on with their lives, so it isn't that bad of a crime. Bullshit."

"Priests aren't supposed to advocate killing, are they?"

I grinned. "I don't have to worry about that anymore."

"Don't you think condemning someone to death is a little harsh?"

I stared at her. She'd never been there. "People like to think that it's easy to recover from things, rape and molestation in particular. That's far from the truth. You think about your sins, whether you believe in God or not. Your body suffers, sometimes surgery is needed to repair things. And people say the molesters have rights? What about the rights of the victims?"

"You really feel powerfully about this. Were you molested?"

I grunted. "No, my sister was."

"How is she now?" Tor asked.

I looked her in the eye. "She's dead. Killed herself when the police let the bastard walk because there wasn't enough evidence."

"How did your parents cope?"

"They didn't. They both drank. My father drank himself to death."

"What about your mother?"

"She lives in a small apartment in a retirement community. She goes to AA, tries to keep straight."

Tor leaned back in her chair. "I had no idea."

"Neither does anyone else. That's what I meant about actions affecting others. The man that raped and molested my sister destroyed her life and broke my family. Ironically, the church was more understanding than anyone else."

"And your view on the church protecting molesters?"

"When I felt safe at church was long before any of that went public. Now I'm disappointed. Kind of glad I left."

"It's a scary world we live in." Tor hugged herself.

"And I don't see it getting better anytime soon."

#

Tabby returned a little after Tor got Will ushered up to their bathroom to get cleaned up. She came through the library door, thumping her arm against the doorframe. "Dammit." Her eyes were sparkling. She rubbed her arm and closed the massive doors behind her. "I found the perfect thing."

A huge part of me wished those doors could lock even though I knew a mere lock wouldn't keep the evil out.

Tabby put the bag on the coffee table in between our sofas. "Ready to see it now?"

I nodded. She pulled a small box out of the bag and handed it to me. It was a black velvet ring box. I stared at her with a raised eyebrow then focused my attention on the box. I opened it, not sure what to expect. There, nestled in ivory silk, was a man's ring. It wasn't an engagement ring or anything, just a ring. Somehow calling it simply a ring, however, didn't fit either. It was a larger man's ring with a Celtic cross in the center. The metal was either white gold or platinum, I wasn't sure which. The cross was bedecked in diamonds and emeralds. It was a beautiful thing, but too much.

"I can't accept this, Tabby," I said.

She smiled back at me. "You don't have a choice, Jimmy Holiday. That's the one that spoke to me when I was looking. Besides, you'd be surprised at how much I paid for it."

I scratched my arm, already feeling the goosebumps rising. No, I probably didn't want to know. I asked anyway. "How much?"

"Uh, uh. No, you don't. Let's say that flea markets are sometimes very good things, and the lady that sold me the ring wasn't sure if the diamonds were real or not."

I sighed. No use arguing. I was stuck. "As long as it didn't cost you much."

"Not much at all." She dug in her bags and placed some candles of various colors on the table. "Now do you want to be here while I work?"

"I'd like to be." And it was true. I wanted to be around her.

"All right then. Give me a piece of your hair and relax. This will take a while."

I plucked a hair out of my head like she asked and handed her both the hair and the ring box. She took her time. Once she began working, I saw colors again. I was getting used to it now. But one thing did cross my mind as I watched Tabby work. What if the colors were the result of whatever Lucy was doing? If I put the ring on that Tabby was fixing for me, would the colors stop?

After she finished, Tabby handed me the ring. I put it on my ring finger and it fit perfectly. The logical part of my mind told me it was coincidence, but my gut told me otherwise. I wasn't the same man. I kind of liked it.

Chapter Twenty-Four

Chrysalis

A HUGE CRASH vibrated along the ceiling. Tabby and I ran upstairs. I heard Will whimpering from Lucy's room. Tor ran down the hall ahead of me. When she reached the door, she jerked it open.

Lucy stood on her bed, the torn restraints hanging from her wrists. Will slumped in the far corner of the room away from Lucy, blood spilling over his face from a gash in his forehead. With his eyes closed and breathing labored, he appeared half dead.

I shouted to Tabby, "Help Will."

Walking over to the foot of Lucy's bed, I stared up at her. Bile collected in my throat, but I pushed the fear aside. It wasn't important. "What did you do?"

She stood over me like a demonic archangel. The light from the window shined in, molding to give her wings constructed from shadows. Her bloody eyes glowed red. Her hands curved into claws. "I gave him the punishment he wanted."

Tabby and Tor crouched next to Will, Tabby checking his pulse.

My heart began to pound faster. I turned all my attention on Lucy. "Uh huh. How did you break the restraints?"

She stared at me with her narrowed bloody eyes. "It's not

like they were very strong."

I wasn't about to argue with her, but the restraints were made of canvas, not something easy to break. I had to be savvy about this, but I didn't know what to do. We needed to get Will out of there without any more damage. I did what I always did when I was at a loss. I winged it.

"All right, Lucy. Are you going to cooperate?"

She let herself fall to the bed and cackled. Her body bounced several times before settling. The *wings* disappeared. "Depends on what you mean by cooperate, Priest."

I snatched a receipt from my pants and grabbed the felt marker from my shirt pocket. I scribbled a list on it. Then I walked over to Tabby and handed it to her. "Take this and get me some supplies." It was worth a shot. Maybe Lucy wouldn't know what was on the list if I didn't make it obvious. "Don't look at the list until you leave the house."

Tabby nodded and ran out of the room. Tor held a towel to Will's head. I nodded at her.

"Are you sure?" She asked me.

"Yes. Go. Help Will."

Will woke up and helped her hold the towel to his head. She eased him to his feet and ushered him out of the room. I closed the door behind them.

I turned back to Lucy.

"You going to fuck me now, Priest?"

I swallowed. This wasn't going to be easy. Not mentally. Not physically. This was going to suck. "No, I'm going to sit here to make sure you don't hurt yourself. You've sent your dad to the hospital, someone has to watch you."

She rolled her eyes in the back of her head and a strange gelatinous substance started coming out of her mouth. It drifted toward the ceiling like smoke badly re-created with CGI. It almost looked plastic.

I'd only seen anything like it in old photographs from the séance craze in the early part of the century.

"The ectoplasm doesn't scare me, Lucy." The sweat on the back of my neck, however, told the truth.

The paranormal blob disappeared and Lucy focused her sickly gaze on me once more. She sat up—her lower body not moving at all. "What does scare you, Priest?"

I smirked at her. "It would be kind of stupid for me to tell you, wouldn't it?"

Shooting me a devilish grin, she said, "I'll find out eventually, so you might as well tell me."

"Hmm....how old are you, really?" I asked. "Lucy's six, but I know you're much older than that."

She rolled her eyes again. "I don't think it matters much, do you?"

"What are you afraid of, Lucy?"

Her smiled widened, her jagged teeth poking out at a painful angle. "I am afraid of nothing. I am oblivion."

I was treading into dangerous territory here, but I had to keep her distracted until Tabby got back. If I asked questions that were normally part of an exorcism, did that put me in the middle of doing one? I had no idea. I was left there alone, grasping at straws.

"You should rest, Lucy. I'm sure you'll want to play more tricks this evening."

She stood back up, but her body did nothing to make it happen. It felt like a video feed had skipped forward, but I was watching her myself, not on a DVD or through a lens. If it wasn't for the fact I was so focused, I think I would have pissed myself.

"If you would stay out of that *room*, I could play lots of tricks." Her voice boomed a thick bass.

"I'm not a big fan of your tricks, Lucy." Shivers were

dancing up my spine.

She laughed darkly. "You are no fun at all."

I heard footsteps pounding up the stairs. Soon after, Tabby opened the door and thrust a bag at me.

"No," I said. "You need to do that part. I'll hold her."

I tackled Lucy on the bed. She bucked beneath me; her hands scratching at any exposed skin. "Keep still, Lucy."

"Fuck you!"

She threw me across the room. Tabby screamed. My body slammed into the wall. I saw stars. My back hurt, but getting Lucy restrained was more important. I pushed myself to get off the floor, took a deep breath and pounced. Throwing Lucy on the bed, I began to pray. Tabby stooped onto the floor, attaching chains.

"The Lord is my shepherd…"

The clinks of the chains echoed through me. Lucy's guttural groans added to the macabre symphony.

"He maketh me to lie down…"

The more I prayed, the stiller she felt.

"Yeah though I walk through the valley of death, I will fear no evil."

By the time the prayer ended, Lucy was outfitted with padded handcuffs from a sex shop and various dog chains fastened to the metal of the hospital bed.

"Okay, it's done," Tabby said.

I rose and stopped my prayers…at least aloud.

"I'll see you dead, Priest."

I stared at her, zeroing in on the thing inside Lucy. I couldn't see it, but I felt it there and to it I spoke. "I'll see you in Hell first."

Tabby pushed me out the door and closed it behind us. She ran her hands over me as if looking for something,

"You're okay?"

"Gonna hurt worse tomorrow, but yeah. Just more bruises."
I followed her down the hall. Lucy had been secured as
humanely as possible. Didn't make me feel any better.

"Where on earth did you find the handcuffs?" I asked as we
descended the stairs.

Tabby snorted. "Tor had them. Apparently, she likes things
a little naughty in the bedroom."

"I didn't need to know that."

"Hey, you were the one who asked."

When we got to the kitchen, Tabby tossed the paper bag
into the garbage. I leaned against the center island and popped
my neck. The pain started to kick in as my adrenaline wore off.

"Tor take Will to the hospital?" I asked.

Tabby nodded. "He needed stitches."

"Well, when he gets here, we can look at the footage."

Tabby sighed and ran her hands over her face. "Can we
contact the church now, please?"

Her voice shook. I'd never seen her this upset.

"Yes, tomorrow." I reached over and took hold of her
hand. It felt right.

#

Tor and Will came home hours later. Will had a bandage
across his forehead. His body slumped, tired and bruised, but
otherwise unharmed.

"What did the doctor say?" Tabby asked.

"That I had a heck of a bump. I don't have a concussion at
least." Will held an ice pack to his head.

"That's good," I said.

"Did you watch the video?"

I shook my head. "We didn't stop the recording, and I'm
glad we didn't. A lot happened after you left."

Will ate some steak Tor set in front of him then wiped his

mouth with a napkin. "I don't know how many more injuries we can take. As it is, the hospital is asking questions. I mean, how are all of us getting hurt this close together? None of this would happen normally. But at least since it's us getting hurt, and not Lucy, they aren't doing anything. Not yet."

I nodded. "I'm getting the church involved tomorrow."

"What about the rest of the evidence?" Tor asked.

"After what happened this afternoon, we've got all the evidence we need. It's not going to be easy for them to ignore it."

After he and Tor finished eating, he ushered Tabby, Tor, and I into the living room. We settled around the TV while Will setup the playback on the security system's DVR.

For a while, everything was calm on the feed. Then Will said something about needing Lucy to be nicer to her mother and Lucy exploded. She rose from the bed like Nosferatu rising from his coffin. Stiff as a board, she simply elevated into a standing position on the bed, the restrains ripping from her wrists and ankles. Will stared at her, his mouth gaping.

"You do not give me orders," Lucy said, and struck Will so hard he flew across the room, hitting his head on the windowsill. His body collapsed into the corner.

Next, it showed us coming in and everything Tabby and I went through getting Lucy restrained again. One thing was different. While I was holding her down, my body blocked her face from the camera. Then, somehow, the DVR showed a close-up of Lucy's mangled face. She grinned into the camera.

"Jesus Christ!" I jumped.

The feed went back to normal a moment later, showing Tabby and I with Lucy in our last exchange.

"That was...disturbing." Tabby rubbed her hands along her arms in rapid strokes.

I took a deep breath. "I think we all better sleep in the

library tonight."

Tabby swallowed. "That's probably a good idea."

We all hunkered in the library with the lights on. It wasn't safe enough for us to sleep in different parts of the house whether I needed a break or not. It was hard to get that image of Lucy smiling at the camera out of my head. My stomach felt like butterflies were tap-dancing inside it.

Tabby and I kept our sofas. Tor took over a sofa that was placed in front of the windows and Will deposited himself in a chair he moved from the other side of the room.

"I think we should take bathroom breaks together," Tabby said.

"That's not a bad idea," I massaged a particularly sore spot along my shoulder, "and a lot cleaner than my idea."

"And that was?" Will asked.

I grinned at him. "A really big bucket."

Tabby hit me with her pillow. "You know, honestly, we should try to all use the bathroom early. Then there will be no one out of this room late tonight."

Everyone went quiet then. I stared at them all in turn. They were trying so hard not to show they were afraid, but I could still see it. Each time the house settled, the level of fear rose with it. I didn't care about the house. Unless it decided to fall on me, it was pretty damn harmless. Lucy-demon-thing, however, was not. I'd learned that the hard way. We all had.

I did my best to not freak out. Enough fear flooded this room and there was no need to make things worse. Demons fed on fear, and I had a feeling that with what happened with Lucy earlier, and the amount of fear hanging around the room, we were in for a hell of a night.

Tor coughed nervously. "Is it wrong to be scared of my own daughter?"

"No, not wrong," Tabby said. "There are plenty of parents

who are afraid of their kids, most though, just have severe behavioral problems. I think with having a possessed child, you have the right to be afraid."

"Try to keep calm," I said. "Demons feed on fear, and the more agitated you become, the stronger you'll make it."

"What are you telling me, Jimmy?" Tor asked.

"I'm telling you that if you can, don't think about your daughter tonight. Everyone needs to stay calm and I want us all to stay in this room. I don't care what noise Lucy makes. The only reason to leave this room is if the alarm on one of her monitors goes off—anything else, do not listen. It is very tricky, this demon."

"When do you think we should get everything?" Will asked.

"Before the noises start."

#

As I expected, things started up about three. Tabby, Tor, and Will had settled into an uneasy slumber. I stayed awake. I couldn't sleep and I couldn't explain it. I could feel it in my gut that something was going to happen.

The pounding began. It started out softly, but gradually grew louder and louder, until I could see something was trying to break Tabby's wards. It was invisible, but each time it started the assault, the wards glowed brighter. At times, they seemed to stretch, almost as if they were about to break. Then the pounding stopped. I looked around. Tor and Will had their blankets tucked underneath their chins. Tabby was sitting up on her sofa. Like me, she seemed to be getting used to this.

A little girl's giggle broke the momentary silence. Tor threw off the blanket.

"Stay still," I said.

The giggle happened again.

She stood up. "If Lucy's okay…"

"Lucy is not okay," I snapped. "This thing plays tricks. It tries anything to get you to leave the confines of this room."

The pounding started again, more vigorously than before. This time, when it stopped, a figure appeared in the doorway of the library—a figure of a little girl with pretty golden hair.

"Mommy?" it said hesitantly.

Tor started for the door, but I snagged her before she reached it.

"It's a trick, dammit!" I shouted at her. "Lucy is upstairs in her room chained to her bed. This thing," I pointed to it, "is a cruel trick."

The little girl disappeared. Tor whimpered.

"Come out, Mommy. I swear I'll be good," the thing said. I couldn't see it, but I could feel it was there, hiding itself.

Tor begged me with silent pleas.

"No."

"What does it want?" she asked.

I stared at her. "Your soul, and I don't think it's above killing to get what it wants."

The little girl appeared in the doorway again, crying. "You don't love me anymore, Mommy."

I kept hold of Tor.

"My baby," she wailed.

I shook her this time as Will and Tabby stared at the figure. "That is not Lucy, Tor. It's an apparition. It's fake."

She struggled and tried to break free of my arms. I glanced over at Will for help. He sat frozen in his chair.

"My sweet Lucy," Tor cried.

I shook her harder. "That is not your baby!"

It pressed its head against the film of the wards.

"These wards only keep out things that mean harm," I said, trying to get her to see sense. "Why else can all of us move freely, and it can't come in?"

The Lucy thing snarled; its face became an exact replica of the Lucy upstairs.

"You can stay there all night, I don't care." She smiled with her broken teeth. "I could always start a fire, you know?"

I laughed. "No you won't. If you destroy this house, you destroy the connection to that ley line."

It giggled. "You are too smart for your own good, Priest."

Then it disappeared.

"Is everything okay now?" Will asked.

"Hell if I know. Tabby and I have had nights that nothing happened. There have been nights with only noises." I ran a hand through my hair. "Then there are nights where the bad things come out. So is this all tonight? I don't know."

Tor and Will searched my face expectantly.

I stared back at them. The weight of the world rested on my shoulders. They had put me on a pedestal. I didn't like it. "Why are you looking to me to save you?"

"Because you're a priest," Tor said.

I sighed. "I'm not a priest. I quit, remember?"

Tabby put a hand on my shoulder. "What if God's rules and the church's rules are two different things?"

I had no answer to that.

#

I watched the night fly by staring out the window. It was calm, but a normal calm. All I saw were trees. Nothing freaky going on outside. Snow covered the ground and ice glinted from the branches. It looked like a Bob Ross winter landscape. I expected more, held my breath for more. Like a ticking bomb waiting to go off, I knew more would come. Maybe Lucy knew the real fight was coming too? Hopefully, I could get someone from the church here soon. If I couldn't, I didn't know how much more we could take. I was exhausted, but sleep wouldn't come.

Tabby's chest rose and fell with every breath. Her sleep was a comfort to me. I knew it wasn't normal. Yet whenever I felt stressed out, watching someone breathe helped relax me. Maybe breathing was a normal function that helped me to focus. Or maybe it grounded me because I knew my sister stopped breathing a long time ago.

I missed Candy. She'd been my protector for so many years; the one who bandaged my knees when they were bloody, and nursed me when I was sick. I hadn't been right since her death. Suicide sucked. I peered back out the window and stared into the night. No one who hadn't been through it could quite understand the feeling of loss when someone killed themselves. When someone who committed suicide died, most people assume it would be the same as when anyone else died. Sadness would encompass you for a while, and then over time, the pain wouldn't hurt the same way anymore. The difference was, when someone committed suicide—they *decided* to die. They made the honest choice to stop living and the rest, those that cared about them, were left wondering what they could have done to keep the one they loved from killing themselves.

"Jimmy?" Tabby asked. "Are you okay?"

I turned around. Something must have woken her up. "Yeah, why?"

"You're crying."

I wiped my hand across my cheek, moisture coated my skin.

"What's wrong?" she asked.

"I was thinking about my sister. That's all. I still miss her, even after all these years."

"How old was she when she died?"

"Eighteen," I focused on the melted snow dripping across the windowpane. "She was eighteen."

Tabby and I watched the sunrise. I could see why Tor chose

the house then. The sunlight danced over the ice on the tree branches. So pretty. The evil of the house didn't match up with the land around it. Black must have made the house the way it was. The land itself wasn't bad. It couldn't be, not to have mornings like this.

Tor woke up not long after the sun finished rising. "That was awful."

"Calm in comparison to some nights," I said.

She nodded. "Do you think it's okay to leave the room now?"

"Probably. Most of the stuff during the day seems to be confined to direct contact with Lucy. I don't know if she's saving her strength for the night, or if some of the things helping her with her tricks are nocturnal."

Tor stretched. "Well then, I'm making omelets for breakfast. Come along, you can pick out what you want."

After we ate, I accompanied Tor to Lucy's room. I was no longer going to let anyone move around the house alone. It wasn't safe—except for the library, where last time I looked, Will was snoring.

When we got to her room, we found Lucy asleep. Her chained arms lay beside her on the bed.

I helped Tor refill Lucy's feeding tube and change the glucose drip on her IV.

We said nothing to each other the entire time. Tor had tears in her eyes when we were leaving, but I paused inside the door. On the other side of the wood, deep scratches had been forced in the grain. They were gouges like someone made them with massive claws. I snapped a picture with my cell phone.

Tor cocked her brow at me in question, but I shook my head. We left the room and closed the door behind us.

"What did you do?" she asked.

"Wait until we get back downstairs."

When we reached the kitchen, I pulled out my phone and showed Tor.

Her hand went over her mouth. Her eyes were wide with alarm. "What caused that?"

I shrugged. "Whatever did it, didn't hurt Lucy. We have other things to worry about."

"Why'd you take the picture then?"

"More proof."

Tabby came in, breaking up our debate. "Will's still asleep."

"Where were you?" I asked.

"Bathroom."

"I thought we agreed we wouldn't go anywhere without anyone else."

Tabby rolled her eyes. "I had to pee, and Will is in there snoring. I couldn't wait, so I went to the bathroom."

With things the way they were, I couldn't help but feel like she took an unnecessary risk.

"So wake up Will," Tor said. "We have things to do. We'll get our showers," she turned to me, "then you are free to do whatever you need to do."

"All right," I said. "Let's get started."

Chapter Twenty-Five

Pain is a State of Mind

IT DIDN'T TAKE too long, not really. Will was sitting in his chair. The blanket had fallen to his waist, but he slept on, snoring lightly.

"Will," I shook his shoulder.

His eyes snapped open.

While he stretched and got settled, I turned on my laptop and browsed for a few minutes. My search landed on the local directory. "What's the name of the Catholic church?"

Will rubbed his eyes. "St. Mary's."

I Googled it and wrote a few numbers. Starting with the first, I counted three rings before it was answered.

"St. Mary's," the voice said.

"Hello." I leaned back on the sofa. "My name is Jimmy Holiday and I could use some help. I need to talk to the priest."

He paused for a moment. "You're speaking to him. I'm Father John. What can I do for you, Mr. Holiday?"

"I'm calling on behalf of a friend. Will Andersen?"

The man coughed. "Yes. How is his daughter?"

"Not doing so well, the treatment at the hospital didn't work."

I could hear him rustling papers. "That's a shame," he said. "Perhaps I can help find another hospital—"

"No, Father. I…," This would be the toughest part, "I really think you need to see Lucy. I don't think she's mentally ill."

He cleared his throat, then a snide tone overtook his calm demeanor. "And what do you think is wrong with her?"

My eyes narrowed. "Maybe you should know that I used to be a priest."

"Really?" I could tell I'd gotten his attention.

"Yes, but that's a story for another day, I'm afraid."

"Maybe today is the day," he said. "Now really, why are you no longer a priest?"

He was starting to annoy me, but if I didn't clarify, he'd assume the worst. "Quite simply, I fell for a girl."

He snorted. "And you defiled your profession—"

Pompous ass. No way, was I letting that slide. "Actually, I did not. My vow of celibacy was true until I left the priesthood, but I think that's enough about me. I want to talk about Lucy."

"All right," he sighed. "Let's talk about Lucy."

"I think she's possessed."

He coughed. "Honestly, Mr. Holiday, you had me going there for a minute."

I let him get the giggle out of his system, before hitting him with the proof. "What six-year-old do you know can speak: Russian, German, Biblical Greek and Latin?"

"What?" he asked. The distinctive sound of sputtering on a drink echoed over the line.

"She displays every sign. I have it all on video."

"Good God." A book slammed shut.

"We need your help."

He coughed again. "I know nothing about exorcism."

"Father, even I know that each diocese is supposed to have its own exorcist. Contact the bishop, and get back to me."

He took my number and promised to get me some word as soon as possible. All I needed was for them to come and investigate, and that was exactly what they would do next. I knew the church too well, much too well.

When the good Father called me back, Tabby and I were sitting at the kitchen table watching Tor pour over several cookbooks. Her therapeutic cooking had hit overdrive since the events from last night.

"Yes, Father." I sat stiffly, ready to fight with him if I needed.

"When do you think it would be convenient for me to visit Lucy and look at the evidence?" His voice shook with the smallest quiver. Had his superior reamed him or was he simply scared?

"Hold on one moment," I said.

I placed my hand over the mouthpiece and spoke to Tor, "Father wants to know when he can come and see Lucy."

"As soon as possible. Whenever he likes." She shivered.

"Anytime would be fine, Father."

The good Father was quiet. "Are precautions in place?"

I chuckled. "Are you asking if she's restrained? Then yes, in fact recently we had to enhance the way she was restrained. You'll see why in what we have to show you."

He clicked his tongue against his teeth. "Is this afternoon too soon?"

"No, Father. The family wishes for someone to help Lucy as soon as possible. This afternoon will work perfectly."

"I'll be by after one."

"Do you remember how to get here?" I tapped my pencil along the table.

"Mr. Holiday, everyone knows how to get to Blackmoor."

Then he hung up. I dropped my phone a little too hard on the table.

"What's wrong, Jimmy?" Tabby asked.

"He called it Blackmoor. The only other person I've heard

call this house that is the local librarian. The name's been used in horror films a lot."

"But not when this house was built," she said.

I stared at her. "Good point. At any rate, he's supposed to be here at one. Where's Will?"

Tor shrugged. "He hasn't left the library. I guess he's going to sleep the day away."

"I'll be glad when I can sleep again."

Neither one of them said anything about that. Unfortunately, just because the priest was coming today didn't mean anything would happen now. We knew we still had nights ahead like last night. But how many?

#

When the priest arrived, we'd all been standing, looking out the front window like a bunch of kids waiting for Santa. It would have been funny if the situation wasn't so dire. Tor had the front door open before the man even reached the walkway.

"Father, welcome," she said. "We're so glad you've come back."

He patted her on the shoulder and allowed her to lead him inside. He was younger than I expected him to be. Not too much older than me. Grey barely flecked his black hair. He was dressed in black with a brown canvas coat.

"Do you want to see Lucy first?" I asked as Will took his coat.

He nodded. "That would probably be best. I take it you're the friend?"

"That's right."

He glanced between me and Tabby for a moment. "Interesting. Very interesting." After his scrutiny, he turned to Tor and Will. "It is best if I see her now. That way, when I ask my questions of her, I am not already biased."

I stayed out of it then. No reason for me to do anything but wait downstairs with Tabby. We heard enough anyway.

"Is he going to believe her?" Tabby asked.

"Believe it or not, this is part of it. The possessed say foul things, do foul things. You've seen the old movies."

She nodded.

"While some of the effects are fantastic, they are pretty realistic. In fact, *The Exorcist* had several priests on staff as consultants."

"Really?"

"Yup. One of them even wrote a book about possession after the movie—"

A thud from upstairs interrupted our conversation. We waited a breath to see if we could hear anything else. Nothing. I searched the ceiling then glanced at Tabby. "I hope he wasn't stupid enough to unhook her restraints."

The priest ran down the stairs. He stopped when he saw us. "Is she always like that?"

I raised a brow at him. "Pretty much. Sometimes she's very violent though."

He nodded. "She threw her father. I don't know how."

"What do you mean?" Tabby asked.

"She threw him against the wall without even touching him."

"So the restraints are still in place?" I asked.

"Oh, yes," he said. "There's little doubt in my mind she's possessed, but I have to see the signs."

Will and Tor came downstairs with Will holding a towel to his nose.

"Want me to help?" Tabby asked Will.

He shook his head.

"You sure?" I asked. When he nodded, I added, "The Father wants to watch the videos."

Will held up his finger for me to wait. He and Tor headed toward the kitchen. We were quiet for several minutes, waiting. When they returned, Will had tape on his nose and it had stopped bleeding.

"She broke my nose," Will said, leading us into the living room. Tabby walked with Tor back to the kitchen. I knew Tor didn't want to see it again, but I had a feeling Tabby was kind of glad she had Tor as an excuse to get out of watching it a second time.

Will cued the DVR to the proper file. As the video showed the peculiar situation, Father John gasped at Lucy's language prowess. The rest, he watched in silence.

"This is very bad," he said when we'd watched all there was.

"When do we hear if she gets an exorcism?" Will asked.

"Sometime soon," the priest said. "I have to let the bishop see the evidence. After that, I should have some sort of answer for you."

Will gave Father John copies of the files on discs. "Call anytime. We don't care what time it is. Lucy needs help."

The priest scratched his head. "I'll do the best I can."

With that, he left, scurrying out of the house like a mouse. The man was deeply scared, but would it be enough?

Chapter Twenty-Six

The Call

I WAS HEADING to the kitchen to get something to drink when my phone rang. I about jumped out of my skin. I scrambled for it, trying to dig it out of my pocket. Almost dropping it twice, I somehow managed to answer it before it went to voicemail. "Hello."

"Mr. Holiday, I'm calling, well, I have some bad news," the voice said. It sounded like the priest.

"Father?" I asked.

He coughed. "Yes, and please, call me John."

I shuffled into the kitchen. The conversation Tabby, Tor, and Will were having ceased.

"Okay, John. Is it all right if I put you on speaker phone?" I sat in the empty chair at the table.

"Yes, that's fine."

I hit the button. "What's going on?"

"The news I have, it isn't good."

I waited for him to say something else. He didn't. "What's the bad news, John?"

He cleared his throat through the phone. "Well, the exorcism's been granted."

Tor gasped then clasped her hands over her mouth.

"That doesn't sound like bad news," I said.

"No. I'm sorry." He paused. "It's been granted, but it's going to be a while before it happens."

"But why?" Tor asked in a voice that was not unlike a squeak.

I heard him sigh. "Right now, in America, we only have about twenty-three exorcists. There's supposed to be one for each diocese, but we don't have them."

"Uh huh," I said. "And how does this affect Lucy's exorcism?"

"There's a waiting list," he paused as if not wanting to say the rest, "I'm afraid the earliest Lucy will get her exorcism will be in about six months."

"She won't last that long!" Tor started to cry.

"Mrs. Andersen, please," Father John said. "I'm doing everything in my power to change that. Times are that hard."

"Is there any way you could do the exorcism yourself, Father?" I asked.

"No, Mr. Holiday. I'm afraid I don't have the training."

I hit the table with my hand. It cracked. This paper pusher was standing in the way. A little girl's life was at stake for crying out loud. "What do you propose we do for six months?"

"Well, if you could take her to Rome—"

"Father, can you imagine Lucy on a plane? She'd attack everyone in sight."

"It was a thought," he said. "In Rome, all you need to do is make an appointment with an exorcist. It's almost like going to the doctor."

"None of that does Lucy any good." I hit myself on the leg. Better to add another bruise than to completely destroy the table.

Will was holding Tor with her head lying on his shoulder. It was the most comforting I'd seen them toward each other.

"Well, Mr. Holiday. You could check with other religions."

"Other religions? Like what?" I asked.

"I believe the Jews have their own form of exorcism. I don't know how well it works."

My mind jumbled and a red haze swam before me, but I didn't know what else to do. Father John had tried, I guess. It wasn't his fault the best he could do was put Lucy on a waiting list, as ridiculous as that sounded.

"Well, keep her on the list," I said. "Maybe God will work a miracle."

"Maybe so," he said.

I hung up the phone. They all were staring at me.

"What?" I asked.

It was Will who first spoke. "You have to do it."

"I have to do what?"

"You have to do the exorcism." He reached over and wiped tears away from Tor's eyes. "You know Lucy won't make it six months. Hell, I don't even know if she'll make it one month."

I knew it was true. There was no avoiding it now. The demon was doing something to Lucy, something I couldn't quite understand, but whatever it was, it was making her sick. If I didn't intervene, she could die. The demon could make sure of it.

"I'm not even a priest."

Tor pleaded with me between tears. "The church said that. I don't know anyone with as good a heart as you have, Jimmy. Please, save my little girl."

What was I going to say to that? Free will could really be a bitch sometimes. I wished I could be told what to do, but it never worked out that way. I wasn't that lucky.

"All right, Tor. I'll do my best," I said, hoping I hadn't made the worst mistake of my life.

#

I went out the back door and around the house to the driveway. God, I needed a break. Tabby followed for some reason. I leaned against her car. "What do you think would happen if I up and left?"

Tabby stared at me and crossed her arms. "To you or to Lucy?"

"Both, I guess."

She sighed. "Jimmy, you've seen Lucy as much as I have. She's not well. Modern medicine is holding off what seems to be the inevitable. What happens if her organs fail again?"

I rubbed my arms. Leave it to stupid me to go outside without my coat with snow on the ground. "Yeah, that isn't something I want to think about."

Fire leapt into Tabby's eyes. Her face flushed. "That's great, Jimmy. If you don't do this, if you didn't try, do you really think you could live with yourself by going back on your word? Let alone if you walked away and later found out Lucy died, waiting for that exorcism."

"What if I make things worse, Tabby? I know nothing about doing this."

Tabby snatched my shoulder and jerked me off her car. "You know what?"

"What?"

"Neither did the first exorcists. They laid their hands on the possessed and spoke to the demons until they got tired. Possession has to do with strength of will. You told me that. Your will has to be stronger than the demon's."

"It's a shame Lucy's 'will' isn't strong enough to protect her." I wasn't this girl's father. Why should it be my responsibility? My insides rebelled. I knew I was being a prick, but I didn't like being cornered without options or a way out. How the hell had I gotten myself into this?

Tabby cocked her head. "Not everyone can be you, Jimmy.

Believe it or not, you're unique."

"I don't know how…" I tried to find another solution, anything. "So I have to do this thing?"

She nodded. "Yep."

"And you'll help?"

"If I can."

I sighed. "All right then, sounds like I better study the ritual. Try to think of spells you can cast on Lucy and her room for light, health, and honesty. Who knows, it might help."

"Any spells you'd like me to cast for you?" she asked.

"Yeah. Luck. It looks like I'm going to need it."

We went back inside and sat at the table. Tor was futzing at the counter, making God knows what. Will sat across from me, nursing a cup of coffee.

"Is there anything I can do to help?" he asked.

I thought for a moment. What I needed him to do and what he was capable of were two different things.

"Honestly, I don't know," I said. "I'm going to need vestments and the rest. Tabby knows what she needs. Mostly, I need something that no one can help me with."

"And what's that?"

"Bravery, hope, strength, luck. Take your pick." I ran my hands through my hair. "I can't promise this is going to turn out okay, Will. I don't know what to do. I don't want Lucy's death on my hands."

Will let out a breath slowly. He seemed old and tired, as if he'd aged twenty years since it all began. "You know, Jimmy, without you, Lucy would have no chance at all." He pushed his coffee cup off to the side and clasped his hands together. "Okay, you don't know what you're doing, but more important is that you care about that. You care about making Lucy worse."

I sighed. He believed in me too much. "I don't want you to put me on a pedestal or anything. I want you to understand.

Once I start this, I don't know what's going to happen. I don't know what Lucy is going to do. I know there's a camera, but I don't want you to blame me if something goes wrong."

"Jimmy," he fisted his hands on the table, "Tor and I have talked about this. Lucy has no other choice. If she dies anyway," he swallowed hard, "well, at least we did all we could, including having you try to get this thing out of her."

"And what if you change your mind? What's going to happen then?"

Will clasped my shoulder. I stared at him.

"We will never blame you, Jimmy. Never."

I jerked away. "You say that now, but people never know how they're going to react."

Will stared at me. "I'm going to be in the room, Jimmy. I'm going to help. How can I blame you if I'm in there doing the same work?"

I had no response to that. He wasn't exactly reliable. I couldn't help but think this was going to be one huge fiasco.

#

Tabby and I set ourselves up in the library early that night, before the others came to bed. Too much to do. I didn't know if I should study the ritual until I had it memorized, or if I should wing it. I swallowed hot water for the umpteenth time. I didn't have the church backing me up. I didn't have the knowledge. Now I wished I had gone to school to be an exorcist.

I tapped my pencil against my lips, staring at a blank piece of notebook paper.

"Are you going to need holy water?" Tabby asked.

I looked up. She was amazingly astute at times. "Actually, yeah. I do need some."

"Does it have to be your type of holy water, or can it be any type?"

I thought for a bit. It wasn't like I was going to be doing this by the book. "Honestly, I don't know. I mean, you always hear about it the Catholic way with the holy water I'm used to, but I have no reason to believe it wouldn't work with any other type. Why?"

She smiled. "Well, you can't get holy water from Father John 'cause he'll suspect. Isn't there something where you can't make holy water now?"

I nodded. "Because I'm not a priest, I can't make 'Catholic holy water.' I'm not supposed to be saying any rituals or masses at all."

"I can make holy water," she said.

I stared at her. It seemed lately Tabby was the answer to everything, but there was still so much about her I didn't understand. "How can you make holy water?"

"Witches and the Voudou do it all the time to cleanse areas and to fight bad things."

I tapped my pencil against the side of my chin. "What do you need to make it?"

"Prayers, rose petals, and vodka."

I dropped the pencil and about swallowed my tongue. "You put vodka in holy water?"

Tabby laughed. "In Voudou, vodka is an offering to Papa Legba."

My mouth froze in a straight line.

"Okay, okay," she said. "Papa Legba is the gatekeeper. Kind of like the equivalent to St. Peter, as far as I understand it."

"So why are you making an offering to this Papa guy?"

She chuckled. "You are so...," she put her hands on her hips when she stood up, "you, Jimmy Holiday. We want the gatekeeper to keep things from coming through the gate, so we put an offering to him in the water."

"Why the rose petals?"

She rolled her eyes at me. "Because, as you well know, roses are related to God. I think there was an old story about roses being the thorns in the crown Jesus wore during the crucifixion or something like that."

"I thought witches didn't believe in Jesus or didn't like Him."

She grinned. "I think we all worship the same being, Jimmy. I don't think the Supreme Being is male or female. I think it is what it is."

"Okay, so, do you have what you need?" I asked.

"Nope. I need rose petals—fresh rose petals, and vodka."

I sighed and settled back into the sofa. "I wish Tor and Will weren't counting on me so much."

"They count on you because they don't have anyone else they can count on."

"Doesn't make it any easier. It's not good, Tab."

She nodded. "No matter what, you have to figure out what you're going to do."

It was more like how I was going to do this. I was stumbling blindly through a field of thorny bushes. "You know my set of instructions equates to like a half-hour worth of prayer?"

"Seriously?" she asked.

"Yeah. I get a half-hour of instruction for something that is going to take weeks probably to deal with, maybe years."

Tabby gasped. "Years?"

"Yes. In Rome, people go to exorcists for years. It's not like how it is in the movies."

"I wish there was another option," she said.

"So do I." I gritted my teeth. "It's going to be dangerous, Tabby. If you want to back out, I'll understand."

"Jimmy, don't go all, 'I'm the man and you don't have to do anything cause I'm here to protect you' on me. I'm here because

I chose to be. You need help. Maybe this is the way it's supposed to be?"

"Maybe," I said.

Tabby and I tried to relax. I stopped pouring over everything. The only thing I seemed to be doing was going crazy.

Tor came into the library carrying a chocolate layer cake.

"What on earth is this?" I asked her.

Will stood sheepishly behind Tor.

"I wanted to give you something, something to thank you," Tor said.

God help me. There was nothing worse than someone making a dessert at a time like this. All I wanted to do was swallow a few Rolaids, not eat a piece of chocolate cake likely to give me a headache.

"How thoughtful," Tabby said to Tor when she saw it.

Tor set the cake on the coffee table. Will grabbed a couple of chairs and brought them over, placing them on either end. Then he put plates, napkins and silverware on the table. Soon Tor had large chucks cut for each of us.

I swallowed bile. I hadn't even eaten dinner, and I didn't want cake, but it was one of those situations where you couldn't refuse. I smiled and choked down my piece. Setting the plate aside as easily as I could, I tried not to jostle. I could only hope my stomach would hold out. Outside it was getting dark.

"When are you going to start?" Will asked.

"Sure as hell isn't going to be tonight." I was trying not to puke. "I feel safer during the day. Besides, Tabby needs to get some supplies before we begin."

Tor's fingers began to shake a bit. Will took her hands to steady them.

This was getting harder and harder. The last thing I needed was to see how badly it was affecting them. If I was selfish, I would have had Tabby try to ward another room, but I couldn't do that.

Tabby looked a little green. The sugar influx hadn't done her any favors either.

Slowly, I sat up on the sofa. "Tor," I said. "As usual you've outdone yourself, but I can't eat stuff like this anymore."

Tor looked like I'd stomped her pet hamster. "I'm sorry, Jimmy. I didn't know you wouldn't like it."

I didn't have the stomach for sensitive anymore. I held up my hand. "That's why I didn't want to say anything. It's not your cooking, it's my stomach. I'm so nervous I'm about to puke, and now I got a slab of chocolate lying in there like a disgruntled wildebeest. It's my stomach, not your food."

Tor relaxed, but looked sheepish. "I cook when I'm nervous."

I raised my eyebrow.

She laughed. "No, I meant to say I cook *more* when I'm nervous."

"Well, I don't care if you cook things for us, but while we are doing this and preparing for it, I'm not going to be able to eat much."

"Why are we always talking about food?" Tabby asked. "I mean, we've got major shit going on, and we're sitting here talking about making food and eating or not eating."

I laughed. "Tabby, I think food is what we've focused on because Tor cooks. Truth be told, we're all trying to avoid the pink elephant in the room as much as possible."

"Well, fuck the food," Tabby jumped from the sofa and walked over to one of the huge windows. "I'm scared, dammit, and it's not okay."

I got up and put my hand on Tabby's shoulder. "You know, it's okay to be scared. I'm scared. Tor and Will are scared. But you know who is the most scared?"

Tabby turned to me. "Who?"

I smiled sadly. "Lucy. She's scared to death. She sees what this thing is doing to her parents. All she wants is to have things go back to normal."

I heard a sob behind me. I turned around to see Tor's head buried in her hands and her chest heaving. I glanced back to Tabby. "You okay?"

"Yeah, I think it caught up with me."

#

Hours later, I reclined on the couch, still awake. It was one of those quiet nights, the ones that really scared the crap out of me because I knew it was building up and saving power for what was next.

I passed the hours reading the Roman Ritual. There was some comfort in reading the prayers, but it left me with a lot of doubts too. The ritual was short, too short. I don't know how the priests before me had managed to do what they did. Being a regular priest was easy. Being an exorcist wasn't. Jesus himself simply laid his hands on the possessed and told the demons to get lost—I wished I was that powerful, but I was just a man.

I drifted off to sleep.

Soon I was standing in the middle of a misty room. I'm not sure if it was a room or an expanse of mist with no walls. I stepped forward and heard a child's laughter, but nothing could be seen in the mist. Then, as if she appeared there, Lucy stood in front of me. The real Lucy. I could feel it was her.

I felt no fear, no nothing. Calm swept over me.

"Hi, Mr. Holiday," she said in a small voice.

I crouched. "Hello, Lucy."

She smiled shyly in the way little girls are apt to do. "He says for me to tell you that no matter what happens, it was meant to be."

It sounded odd coming from her mouth. She didn't sound like a six-year-old, but not in the demonic way. This was different. "He who?"

She grinned broader. "You know."

I shook my head and she returned it with a knowing look. Then she wandered off into the mist.

"Lucy, don't go," I called after her.

Very faintly, I heard her sing. "Jesus loves the little children..."

I jerked awake. The only sound to be heard was the ticking of the clock in the hallway.

Chapter Twenty-Seven

Beginnings

THE NEXT MORNING, Tabby and I traveled to find her supplies for the exorcism. It took about thirty miles to locate the place Tabby had seen on the internet—some sort of special new age store. I didn't mind. If it helped Lucy, what did I care? The items I needed for the exorcism — the vestments and everything else — had appeared on my sofa in the library. I didn't question how they got there. I knew I hadn't somehow packed them in my bag and then forgot. I hadn't had any of the garb in my possession since I'd left the priesthood. Was it divine intervention or something else? I had no one to ask. The only person who had been with me in the house had been Will and he definitely didn't have access to the garb. This one, I took on faith.

Tabby pulled into the parking lot of the store called "Pyewackett." I didn't ask.

I fiddled with my shirt and stared off into space as Tabby went in to gather her supplies. I was trying to gear up for what I had to do later. It wasn't as cold so I didn't bother turning the car back on.

Rap! Rap! Rap!

An old man with long greasy white hair stood beside the car, dressed in a caftan. He looked like something right out of the sixties.

I rolled down the window a bit. "Can I help you?"

The man shot me a cool grin. "You got the mark."

I blinked. What the hell? "What?"

The man pointed at me. "*You* got the mark."

I patted my body and gazed over every exposed piece of skin, but saw nothing. "The mark of what?" The guy wasn't playing with a full deck. His grin, I was sure, couldn't get any wider, but somehow it did.

"You know, *the mark*." The man gestured with his fingers like he was going to say "oogie boogie." "You can see the colors no one else sees. You witness the writing in the air no one feels, and you hear the noises others fear to hear. You got the mark."

I raised an eyebrow. "How do you know I have, 'the mark?'

He grinned again. "We markers know other markers."

I sighed. This kook was pretty damn different. Now how he knew I could do any of that, I had no idea. And this mark thing made no sense. "What do 'markers' do?"

He stared at me, his smile dropping into a stoic mask. "You'll see."

With that, he raced away as if the Devil were on his heels.

I jumped out of the car, trying to follow him. Running around the building, I kept trying to catch up, but something seemed to stop me. When I got to the back, I searched everywhere. He should have been there. He wasn't.

I ambled to the car, catching my breath. As if I didn't have enough on my plate, now I had psychos telling me I was part of some weird secret society. I wanted to chalk it all up to a ration of bullshit, but I couldn't do that. There was no way he could have known about what I could see. No plausible explanation for that at all.

A piece of paper stuck out from under Tabby's windshield

wiper. It read, "Jesus Saves."

"This is getting ridiculous," I mumbled.

I climbed inside and slumped in the passenger's seat. Soon Tabby came out with a large bag.

"Got everything you need?" I asked.

"I think so."

I didn't bother telling her anything about what had happened. It was all too unbelievable. And I had much more important things to worry about—like the soul of a little girl.

"Do you smell something?" Tabby asked.

I sniffed, there was a foul odor. "Yeah, it doesn't smell good."

Tabby got back out of the car and walked around to the front of it. "Sweet Cartwheeling Jesus!"

I rolled down my window. "What?"

"Somebody shit in front of my car! How did you not notice?" She stared at me, her eyes darkening.

I jumped out. "It must have happened when I was gone."

She shot me a glare. "Gone? Where were you?"

I sighed. "I guess I wasn't paying attention. There was this guy... I don't know."

Tabby grumbled and buckled into the driver's seat. "You really are ridiculous sometimes, you know that?"

I kept quiet. Now was not the time to explain about the man, and there was a part of me, a pretty large part, that knew it was possible he'd taken a dump in front of the car. How had I missed the smell?

We rode back to the house in silence. I wanted to tell Tabby the truth, but it was bad enough I was distracted by the whole thing. I didn't need her distracted too.

"Hungry?" she asked.

"Yeah, kinda."

She seemed relaxed, her anger gone. "No offense to Tor,

but I'm getting tired of gourmet food."

I snickered. "So what are we getting?"

"Grease. Something with lots of grease."

#

When we pulled into the drive of the house after our grease filled meal, I gripped her arm gently.

"What?" she asked.

"How long will it take you to make the holy water?"

She cast a lopsided smile at me. "How long did it take you to make holy water?"

I shrugged. "I dunno. A few minutes anyway. The prayers took more time."

"Same here, except I have to crush the rose petals and add vodka."

"Vodka. If the church could see me now."

Tabby snorted. "It could be worse."

I couldn't imagine it getting any worse. "How so?"

She hopped out of the car and snatched her bag. I followed.

"I could be telling you to piss on a coconut and kick it out the front door yelling, 'Get the fuck out of my house!'"

I stared.

She grinned. "See?"

When we came in, Tor was sitting at the kitchen table, coffee cup at her side, reading the Bible. Of all the people I would have expected to be reading the Bible, Tor wasn't it.

"Where's Will?" I asked.

She glanced up from the book. "Getting drunk in the library."

Tabby set her bag on the table. I stayed where I was—right near the counter.

"Did something happen?" Tabby asked.

Tor wiped at her eye. "We went to fix up Lucy's feeding

tube."

I left the protection of the counter and stepped forward. "Okay."

"Lucy was levitating."

"What? How?" Tabby asked.

"I could see underneath her body when I changed the bag for her feeding tube. She...she was levitating as far as the chains would let her."

I nodded. "So why is Will getting drunk?"

Tor slammed her Bible shut. I winced.

"Because he's an asshole! 'Can't take it,' he said." She pushed the book across the table. "Am I the only one that sees that there's a huge problem if he's supposed to help with the exorcism?"

I sat in the chair beside her. Tabby started unloading her bag to make the holy water.

"If he's drunk, he's not going in that room," I said. "He'll be vulnerable, and that sets him up for possession. I'm not taking that chance."

"That means I have to do it," Tor said. "Damn him."

I shook my head. "You don't have to be there. I'm doing the exorcism now. Tabby is going to be there. If you want to see, you can watch the monitor on the security system."

Her shoulders slumped. "Thank God." She got up, gripped her Bible, and stowed it in a drawer in the center island.

"Do you have a large pot I can use?" Tabby asked, holding up the roses. "Making holy water."

Tor pulled a large stock pot out of the pantry. "This okay?"

It was the biggest damn stock pot I'd ever seen, something meant for restaurant use.

"That's perfect." Tabby's eyes widened with excited energy.

Tor handed it to Tabby and turned to me. "Why aren't you making the holy water?"

I smiled. "I'm not a priest."

Tor sighed. "I'm going to pretend that makes sense."

She sat in her chair while Tabby got to work. It went pretty quickly, at least the mixing of water, vodka, and rose petals. Then the prayers began. Tor watched, seeming fascinated. I was interested too, but for a different reason. With each prayer or spell she recited, I saw a layer of color appear on the holy water then slowly fade away. It brought me back to this *mark* thing. I couldn't ignore it. When Tabby stopped her ritual, I decided I needed to talk.

"Have you ever been to that store before?" I asked her.

Tabby raised her eyebrow at me. "Why?"

"While you were inside, this old guy with long hair spoke to me."

Tabby giggled. "What?"

"Never mind," I said.

"Okay, weird old guy, check," she said. "Keep going."

"He talked about things. Stuff with magic." I sighed. "He said, and I quote, 'You have the mark.'"

She pursed her lips together. "What mark?"

"That's just it, I don't know."

"Jimmy, after all of this is over, I think you need a nice holiday."

I slumped in my chair. "I don't even know why I bother."

Tabby patted me on the head. "Be a good little exorcist and get ready."

#

Climbing the steps to Lucy's room as an exorcist was far different than before. It was like the mere thought of what I was about to do was so oppressive I could hardly breathe.

I reached into my pants' pocket. Yes, my rosary was there. In my other side, there was a flask of holy water—it was the best I'd been able to do under the circumstances. Over the top of my regular clothes, I wore the vestments and the purple stole. Like a kid dressed up for Halloween. When the clothes appeared, I hadn't put much thought into it. And no one at the house even had access to a church to get them. I chalked it up to someone, maybe the real Lucy, trying to help me.

I looked ridiculous, hell I felt ridiculous. Here I was, wearing a suit coat borrowed from Will, a white T-shirt, and a pair of jeans. Over this I wore a collar and a purple stole. I felt like a clown.

Strange growls seemed to float along the walls as Tabby and I walked. I paused in the middle of the staircase.

"What's wrong?" Tabby asked.

"I'm supposed to confess before the exorcism."

"Does it have to be to a priest?"

I laughed a little. "We're not exactly doing this by the book anyway."

She nodded. "Okay, what do you have to confess?"

I sighed. "I've had impure thoughts about you. I've been angry with Will because of his weaknesses, I've been short of patience with Tor, and I have wanted to run from this."

She smirked then forced the smile away. "Is that all?"

"Yes."

"Okay, you've confessed. Let's go."

I took a deep breath and started back up the stairs. The sounds continued. Then, a smell so foul I gagged met us on the landing. It was sulfuric and had an undertone of rotten meat.

"What is that?" Tabby asked.

"The smell of the demon." I'd been so sure when we started the climb. "It does these things to show us its power. It wants us to doubt our abilities."

"Don't listen to it," she said.

"I won't. Neither should you."

When we got to her door, I stopped and turned to Tabby. "Bow your head."

She stared at me, but didn't question it. I closed my eyes.

"Saint Michael, the Archangel, defend us in battle; be our defense against the wickedness and snares of the devil. May God rebuke him, we humbly pray; and do thou, O Prince of the heavenly host, by the power of God, thrust into Hell Satan and the other evil spirits who prowl about the world for the ruin of souls. Amen."

"Amen," Tabby said quietly.

I took a deep breath then turned and opened the door to Lucy's room. She was levitating against the chains.

"Hello, Priest," Lucy said.

Tabby and I stepped inside. It was cold enough to see our breath, and yet, Lucy was covered in sweat.

"Hello, Lucy," I said.

"Lucy isn't here anymore, Mr. Holiday," it said. "But you already knew that."

Tabby and I sat on the floor around the bed.

"I don't know if Lucy is in there or not, but I have faith that she is."

It cackled. "Poiba Toohnyet sgoloveh."

I shook my head. "I don't speak Russian."

It grinned. Its bloody eyes seemed to glow. "Shall I translate for you?"

"Yes."

"A fish rots from the head down. God is dead, we are in power now."

I grunted. "Lies, demon. All you can do is tell lies."

It laughed again. "I have more truth than you know."

I began to pray. "Our Father who—"

It thrashed against the bed. "Fuck you! Fuck you!"

"Art in Heaven. Hallowed be thy name! Thy Kingdom

come! Thy will be done on Earth as it is in Heaven!"

It snarled and spat at Tabby. A blood clot landed on her face. She grimaced, but wiped it away with a tissue.

"Give us this day our daily bread. And forgive us our trespasses as we forgive those who trespass against us. Lead us not into temptation, but deliver us from Evil. Amen."

Lucy flopped around on the bed. Her eyes rolled into the back of her head. Her mouth hung open. And then, diarrhea began spilling from her mouth onto the floor.

"Is that possible?" Tabby asked.

"Normally no, but this is the demon."

It laughed. "Your sister said to tell you, 'Hello.'"

I froze then whispered, "How is she?" Stupid. I shouldn't have asked, but it slipped out. Dammit. I needed to be more careful.

It smirked, poor Lucy's brown teeth rotted to black. "She's hanging around."

There was no way Lucy could have known my sister hanged herself, no way in hell. The demon struck low and hard. I refused to be swayed from saving Lucy.

"What is your name?" I asked it with as much force as I could muster into the question.

It let loose a horrendous howl of laughter. "You didn't think it would be that easy, did you?"

The feces disappeared. It had all been a parlor trick. "Cheap tactic."

Lucy's eyes snapped toward me as if it knew exactly what I was thinking. "You don't want to get me angry now, do you?"

I changed courses. "Is Mr. Black around?"

It smiled again. "He's around. She's around. We're all around."

Tabby waved for my attention and pointed to the Roman Ritual.

I had lost my place. I didn't know what I was doing. I was in way over my head. I got up and placed a hand on Lucy's forehead.

"I exorcise you, Most Unclean Spirit!"

It cackled at me again. "You are pathetic."

"What is your name?" I couldn't give into it. Tabby put her hand on my shoulder.

I stared down the demon, willing it to do what I wished.

Lucy turned her head toward me. "I am the one who has control. I am the one who feeds, feeds on the flesh and the blood of the life while you are the one who bleeds."

I threw holy water across the demon in the shape of the cross. Blisters appeared on Lucy's skin where the water hit. There was a sound so strange, I didn't know what it was at first. Then I identified it and my heart sunk. It was the sound of a child crying.

I glared at the demon inside the child. "What is your name?"

"I want my mommy!" It wailed.

I'd been waiting for this trick. Too soon, too easy. I crept closer to the bed. "What is your name?"

It tried to punch me, but I wasn't close enough.

"What's wrong?" I purposefully antagonized it. "Used too much energy?"

It growled so loud it shook the house. "Lucy goosy likes to eat pussy." It grinned at me with the sweetest of smiles. The bloody eyes and the black teeth spoiled that effect.

"When are you going to stop playing this game, Black?"

It stared at me.

"I'm not stupid you know," I said. "You are the flesh eater, you are the one who likes to make people bleed."

"Oh you silly thing," it said. "I was in Mr. Black. His soul is long gone."

"How am I to believe that, if you haven't given me your name?"

"Tricky, tricky." Then it closed its eyes and pretended to sleep.

Tabby and I left the room.

"Round one over, I guess," I said.

"What do we do next time?" Tabby asked.

"Same damn thing. That's what an exorcism is, a battle of wills between the demonic and the exorcist."

"So what do we do now?" she asked.

"Prepare for round two."

Chapter Twenty-Eight

Take Two

AFTER A BREAK, Tabby and I headed upstairs again. No foul smell permeated the air this time. I opened the door and switched on the overhead light. Lucy was sitting up in bed. She watched us come into the room with those awful eyes of hers. The blood overtook all the white, leaving dark black pupils and circles of red.

"Good evening, Lucy," I said.

"Where am I, Jimmy?" she asked, but it wasn't Lucy's voice, and it wasn't the demon's.

"Who are you?"

Lucy buried her head in her hands. "How could you? You let him do this to me. Why?"

Then I knew. The damn demon was copying again. It was pretending to be my sister. While that sank a cold, hard pit in my gut, it bothered me more that the demon was resorting to using tricks again. It was old and redundant. And it pissed me off.

"Candy is dead, Lucy," I blinked away the tears that were already forming.

It smiled. "But she's with us, Priest. She's always been with us. Suicide is a direct trip to Hell."

I stepped backward. The blood drained from my face and

my palms started to sweat.

It laughed.

I motioned for Tabby to sit. She did. I followed. We took position at the end of the bed on the floor, facing Lucy. It was time for the real fight to begin.

"One, God does not punish the mentally ill. Two, give it up. You are more original than that."

"But you can't be sure," she said in a sing-song voice.

"Candy has been gone for almost twenty years. The Candy I knew was dead before she killed herself."

"If you let us take you, you could see her again."

"I can see her anytime I want. She's here," I patted my chest. "I remember her."

"And you," it turned to Tabby, "don't you think God is overjoyed an itchy witch is trying to chase me out. Evil can't move evil."

"I'm not evil," she said.

It cackled. "You know the words, 'Thou shalt not suffer a witch to live!'"

Tabby's eyes narrowed. "Too bad that was a poor translation. The original text doesn't say that at all. That passage talks about charlatans who charge money. They want to bilk people out of their riches by proclaiming to know the future or do spells for them to make them wealthy. It doesn't apply to me."

"Oh really?" It moved the index finger of her right hand around. An image appeared, hovering over her head. "Itchy witchy thinks she's smart. She thinks she's good at heart, but her heart is marred by the devil's lie, making her sure to die." As she said the riddle, a little Tabby replica walked across the bed until a large hand squashed her to nothing.

"That isn't scary," Tabby stood stoically.

I was proud of her.

"Not scary?" The hooded figure appeared, looming over her.

Tabby jerked away and backed up. It floated across the floor toward her.

I rose and blocked its path. "Back."

It paused.

"Back," I said. I held my hand high. A beam of green light shot out of my palm and wound around the dark figure like a rope. It surprised the hell out of me, but I kept going. I had to protect Tabby. I had to save Lucy. I couldn't stop. "You will do no more bidding for the thing that lives inside Lucy. Back!"

The figure rippled and disappeared.

"Jimmy, what the hell?" Tabby asked.

"I'm..." I stared at my hand where the light had radiated only moments ago. The man in the parking lot, his words came to my mind. It was true. "I'm a marker."

It squealed like a pig.

I had the upper hand. Time to use the advantage. "What is your name?"

It flopped on the bed and rolled around.

Tabby took me by the shoulder. "We need to talk later."

It sat back up. "Talk now, I won't bite."

I sighed, no longer afraid. Strength flowed through me like water. "You know, you're a little pedantic."

It flung me across the room without touching me. My head hit the wall, the pain crushing. My sight dimmed.

"You stop that!" Tabby snatched a pouch from her pocket. "You evil--" She threw holy water on it.

It screamed.

I sat up, my head swimming. It was attempting to fling Tabby like it'd done to me, but somehow Tabby remained rooted to her spot. I could see red light bouncing off her. I focused on it and attempted to stretch my power toward her.

"No!" Tabby yelled.

I stopped.

"Don't link with her mind, it will get you," Tabby said.

While Tabby's attention focused on me, it threw Lucy's IV pole at Tabby, hitting her in the head.

Tabby cried out. A gash opened on her forehead. Blood ran into her eyes. She fell over unconscious.

I jumped up and sprung over to Tabby. She went still. I felt for a pulse, grateful to find one, but the fear rose in me like prickling pins. I had to push it down.

I glared at the demon. "You son of a bitch!"

It smiled. "Not nice words for a priest."

I stood up and smacked it across the face. "I'm not a priest!"

The whole room shook. It felt as if the earth shifted and then righted itself again. I fell and covered Tabby's body with my own.

Someone knocked at the door.

"Don't come in, whatever you do, don't come in."

They ignored me. Will came bursting into the room, staring at Lucy. "I came to take Tabby to the Emergency Room. I saw everything on the monitor."

The shaking ceased.

It let us leave the room with Tabby. After Will and I got Tabby into the car, I went back in with Tor and helped her clean up Lucy's broken IV and fix the feeding tube for the night. The entire time, it watched me with a huge grin on its face.

Before we left the room, it said, "You're all alone now, Priest."

I shut the door.

Chapter Twenty-Nine

Solution

1950

"IT'S HAPPENED BEFORE, you know?" the demon said.

The old priest stood up straighter, his wizened hands hanging loosely at his sides. "What is it you are referring to?"

The darkness of the room drifted into one corner. The bookcase behind was visible now, and the silver objects glowed with a faint blue light. "Many have tried and failed, Priest."

The old priest reached into the breast pocket of his coat and pulled out a flask of holy water.

"Do you really think that will hurt me?" it asked.

The priest threw the water on the darkness in the corner of the room. Wind began to blow, tossing books from the shelves.

The priest searched the room—and then, a hand landed on his shoulder. He whipped around. Mr. Black's ruined face stared at him. "You didn't think it would be that easy, now did you?"

The priest swallowed. "This will not scare me. There is nothing frightening about the dead."

The broken face smiled at him. "And the undead?"

The black mass surrounded the priest and covered him. The pain was massive, like a large pole rammed down his throat. He didn't even have time to scream.

The priest's body slumped to the floor. The visage of Black disappeared. The darkness disintegrated. The laughter ceased.

Chapter Thirty

Come What May

TOR AND I sat in the kitchen. She couldn't stop moving around. When she'd gotten up and wiped the counter for the fourth time, I couldn't take it anymore.

"Stop," I said. "You're making me nervous."

She plopped down at the table. "I'm so sorry about Tabby."

I nodded. "She'll be okay. Will called and told me she came to on the way to the hospital. If they don't release her tonight, they will tomorrow."

"I didn't mean for anyone to get hurt," she said.

"It could be worse. At least she wasn't seriously injured." I was beyond thankful that the thing inside Lucy hadn't killed her. I had had about enough of all of this. Things had changed. It had hurt someone I loved.

I pulled out my phone and checked for a text from Tabby, but there was nothing.

Tor sighed. "My Lucy's going to die, isn't she?"

I grabbed Tor's hand. "Stop talking like that. We know nothing. I'm doing what I can. If it doesn't work, you can wait for the church's exorcist."

Tor covered her mouth with her hand and cried out. "I don't think she'll last that long."

"When is her next CAT scan?"

"I canceled it. I can't risk anyone else getting hurt."

#

When Will came back with Tabby in tow, I jumped up and hugged her. I couldn't help myself.

Tabby coughed. "I need to breathe sometime."

I let her loose and chuckled.

"She's supposed to stay awake for the next twenty-four hours to make sure she doesn't have a concussion. The tests were inconclusive," Will said.

"That won't be a problem." I pointed my finger at Tabby. "No more exorcism for you."

Tabby jumped up. We had to grab her as she almost fell.

"Dammit, Tabby," I said. "You got hurt. Enough already."

"But don't you need witnesses?"

I put my hand on her shoulder. "I have the camera. All three of you can watch the feed. That's three witnesses."

"No more tonight," she said.

"No, not tonight. I'm going to keep you up for twenty-four hours. Lucy can wait."

Tabby looked me in the eyes. "I hope so."

We all hunkered in the library for the night.

Tabby sat on the sofa. "What do you think is going to happen tonight?"

I scratched my head and finished chewing. "I don't know."

Will and Tor were listening, but they had sequestered themselves to the other side of the library playing chess. I glanced over. Even though they looked like they were playing, I could tell that they were listening to the conversation—no one had made a move.

"What are you going to do?" Tabby asked.

I shrugged. "The best I can, I guess. I mean, it's not like I can do anything else."

"Well, tomorrow we'll—"

"No," I glared at Tabby. "You are not going back in with it. I don't care if I have to drag Will in there whining like a baby. You are not going."

Tabby shook her head. "How else are you to trap the demon, genius?"

She had a point. I was flying by the seat of my pants. The only thing I seemed to know how to do was piss the demon off. I hadn't gotten it to do anything, let alone tell us its name.

"I could always move the site of the exorcism," I said. The energy in the room increased and seemed to crackle around us.

"What are you talking about?" Tabby asked.

"I could move the exorcism into the attic."

It seemed like time stopped. I could hear nothing, no wind outside, no ticking of the clock, I couldn't even hear them breathe.

"What?" I asked.

Tabby stared at me. "That's either the stupidest thing you've ever said, or you are a freaking genius."

I sighed. "The way I figure it, if I manage to get it out of Lucy, then it will jump the ley line and get the hell out of here."

"What if Lucy brings other things in?"

"That hasn't stopped it in her room. I don't see what difference that would make in the attic. Anyways, I can do the green ball thing."

Tabby stared at me like there was something wrong with me. "What green ball thing?"

I pointed. "Up in Lucy's room, the hooded thing. You didn't see it?"

"Oh, I saw the hooded thing all right. I saw you yell at it until it left. I saw no green ball thing."

I scrunched in my chair. "That must be my marker stuff."

Tabby sighed at me. "I think you are losing your mind, I

really do."

"Tabby, when was I ever sane?" I chuckled.

She grinned. "Good point."

"The marker stuff. Even I don't know what it is exactly. That old guy—the one that probably shit in front of your car, talked about the things I'd been doing lately."

She raised an eyebrow. "What things?"

"Seeing the colors of your magic."

#

Will and Tor went to sleep sometime before eleven. Tabby and I sat on her sofa, reading. I looked up now and again to make sure she was still awake. So far, there had been no problems. She seemed okay, and I was thankful for that.

Finally, Tabby caught me staring at her. She peered out over the top of her book. "Are you really going to do it?"

"Yeah," I said. "I think it's reached the point of no return. Even if I quit now, the demon knows us and would try to come after us someday."

"How are you going to do it this time? Are you still going to use the Roman Ritual?"

"No. It doesn't seem to be working too well for me. I can't do parts of it and I don't feel right wearing the vestments. You kind of need those to do it the Catholic way."

"Why don't you feel comfortable?" She set her book on the coffee table.

"Once you give up the priesthood, you can't wear the uniform. Think about a cop who is no longer a cop. They aren't supposed to wear the uniform. It's against the law, considered impersonating a police officer."

Tabby tapped her chin. "Well, maybe you need a different ritual."

"And where am I going to find that?"

"You don't have to. We're going to write one." She leaned over and dug around in her bag. She came up with a notebook and pen.

I sat up, my book dropped to my lap. "We are?"

"We are. To do magic you don't need a special outfit," she said. "A lot of people work skyclad."

I raised an eyebrow. "Is that what I think it is?"

Tabby smiled.

"I am not doing an exorcism nude."

She laughed. "I don't expect you to. Clean clothes will do."

"All right, what else?"

"Evidence of the four corners. North, south, east, and west. Earth, air, fire, and water."

"I don't know about this."

She snorted. "It's better than your plan of winging it."

I felt sheepish as hell. She'd nailed me. I had nothing left. I was intending to yell at the demon. "Okay, I'll trust you."

#

When it was my turn to sleep, it didn't take long to crash. The dream began as a scene. I was in the kitchen of Blackmoor. The cabinets were wooden with crisscrossed slats over the glass so you could see the china inside. In the center of the room, a large rectangular table stretched the length of the kitchen. There was no center island. A baby sat in an old fashioned wooden high chair.

A pretty brunette was running around the kitchen, fixing something. She stopped, almost like she sensed me. Bruises circled both of her eyes. She was as thin as a corpse and the severe black dress she wore did nothing to take away that impression. Holding her finger to her lips, she whispered, "Shhh. It will hear you."

Spinning wildly, she finally centered on me. Her walk was in fits and starts—like she would appear at different points as she moved forward. She pointed toward the ceiling.

"Don't take her there."

"Why?" I asked.

"You know."

I jerked awake. "Jesus Christ."

#

When I woke up a second time, Tor and Tabby were sitting on the sofa, watching me sleep.

I rose. "What time is it?"

"About six," Tor said.

I got up, went over to the chair where Will was sleeping and kicked his foot.

His eyes popped open.

"Come on, bucky. We've got work to do."

He sat up, wiped the sleep out of his eyes and stood.

"Let's go," I said.

We made a stop at the garage so Will could get some tools. Then we headed upstairs. Lucy's room was cold, but there were no foul smells, no sounds. Lucy appeared to be sleeping. Will and I dismantled the camera system. She never woke. We left the room and closed the door.

"That was uneventful," Will said.

I hit him on the arm. "Don't jinx us."

We headed toward the attic, flipping on lights as we went. The covered furniture inside looked like an army of ghosts. Of course the bulb was burned out to the little room. I took a deep breath and opened the door to what was going to become my battlefield. This time, instead of magical artifacts scattered around the room, I saw projectiles Lucy could throw at me. "I need a big box."

"Why?" Will asked.

I pointed around the room. "Too much stuff."

Will set the camera equipment aside, grabbed a box, upended it, and dumped the contents onto the floor.

After that box and two others, we had all of the crap out of the room.

Sweat dripped off my brow. Will wasn't in much better shape.

"Let's do this," I said.

We hooked up the camera, and after a few trips downstairs, we got the wireless feed working properly.

"Fuck, I need more sleep."

Will stared at me. "You don't have to do this today, you know?"

"Yeah, I do. I don't want to drag it out any longer than it needs to be."

"You could take a nap," he said.

I chuckled. "No need. If I don't make it, I'll get all the sleep I'll ever need."

As I walked to the library, I remembered I had used my last set of clean clothes the day before. When I entered the room, I found my clothing out of my bag, clean, and folded on my sofa. They must have done them while Will and I were getting the camera fixed. "Thank God for women."

I changed clothes, grasped the items Tabby had set out for me—a bottle of holy water, a feather, a candle, and a rock. I put the pages of the ritual we had written in my pocket. I yawned. I didn't know what to make of that dream. Could that have been Mrs. Black? The one who'd been eaten. Warning me away from the room was kind of sweet in a way for a ghost, but I had no choice anymore.

I knelt in front of the window. "Heavenly Father, give me the strength to do this. If someone has to die, let it be me. Lucy has a whole life to live."

And then, I heard a whisper. "It will be all right, Mr. Holiday."

The voice, the whisper, it was the same I had heard days before. It was the voice of Lucy—her true voice.

I took a deep breath and left the room. After this, if I survived it, I was going to need therapy.

"Got any hooks we can screw into the floor?" I asked.

After a trip to the garage again, we had our supplies. "Where do you want it?"

I pointed to the far corner. We screwed the latch to the floor. The steel end flipped up so that the chains could be passed through it.

I grabbed the mirror from outside the room and put it inside the door.

"Ready to get Lucy?" Will asked.

"As ready as we'll ever be," I said.

We got into Lucy's room as she was waking. When her father walked to the side of her bed, her eyes went wide.

"What are you doing?" it asked.

I smiled. "We are taking you where you want to go."

"And where is that, Priest?"

I smiled. "To the room in the attic."

It visibly relaxed. "You'll have to take the chains off the bed to do that."

I nodded. "Yes, but remember if you do anything to either one of us, you can't make it to the attic room."

Its eyes narrowed then relaxed. "As you wish."

Chapter Thirty-One

Sweet Release

I UNDID THE chains from Lucy's handcuffs. They clinked in a way that sounded final. It wasn't a usual sound, more like an old iron gate being closed. Will detached Lucy's feeding tube, took her in his arms, and walked out. I followed behind with the chains. Lucy kept her word. She was completely docile, allowing Will to carry her without any problems. When we entered the attic, Will let me go first. I attached the chains to the latch screwed to the floor. I doubled them up so Lucy couldn't get too far. We set Lucy on the floor while I attached her handcuffs to the chains.

Will stepped away.

"Do you want to stay?" I asked. His face turned pasty white and dripped with sweat.

Will shook his head. "How long do you think this will take?"

"I don't know. About an hour or two."

The demon's laughter encompassed the room.

"All right." He left, closing the door behind him.

I stared up at the camera. The green light was on, indicating it was recording. This was it. The nervousness in my stomach made my guts rumble. I turned to peer at the demon inside

Lucy. It was sitting up, smiling sweetly—or what it considered sweet. It looked damn freaky to me like a lion about to pounce on an antelope.

"Why do you like this room so much?" I asked.

It snarled at me. "It is a place of power."

My heart began thumping in my chest. I could feel the vibration through my sternum. I took a deep breath and pulled the items out of my pocket.

The room was bright. The early morning sun shone through the dormer windows. At least, due to the sun, I could tell where east was. I set up my magic circle with salt the way Tabby had told me to do, doing my best to make a semi-correct circle on the floor with me in the middle.

Numerous clawing sounds skittered around the walls. The scratching echoed. I paused. The circle was not complete yet, and the theatrics were already beginning. For a moment, I wondered if there was more than one demon in Lucy, and then I remembered—Lucy was a mimic.

"You don't think that circle will save you, do you?" it asked.

I stared at it. Again, it was smiling. I finished the circle, ignoring it. I set the items where the four corners should be and began calling the corners in the clockwise fashion.

It rolled its eyes at me. "You're doing it wrong. Widdershins is most powerful."

I shook my head. This demon was trying to get me to do evil. Tabby had explained to me that counter-clockwise was the way of black magic.

"Who are you?" I asked.

It smiled. "You know my name. It's in your book."

I sat in the middle of the circle, and brushed the excess salt off my hands. "Which book?"

It snarled. "Your religion."

This thing was so entrenched in Lucy, it couldn't even say

anything holy—anything to do with God. "Okay, you mean the Bible?"

It spat a gob of bloody phlegm at me. The mucus didn't reach. It bounced off the invisible shield of the circle, except it wasn't invisible to me; it glowed a pale blue.

My heart hammered hard in my chest. *Lub Dub. Lub Dub. Lub Dub.* The electricity rose in the room. I had to begin.

"Hail to the guardians. Guardians of light, strength, hope and peace. Hear my call."

It snarled. The room shook with a massive rumbling. "This is boring."

The floorboards groaned.

I paused. When nothing else happened, I continued, "By the power of three times three, save this little girl. Send her soul back to her, back to the light. Expel the dark one. Bind him, hold him, keep him from others for a thousand years."

It growled. The walls creaked and rattled. My bottle of holy water fell over. The sunlight had dimmed. Almost like darkness was taking over the room. The sun was trying to come through, but the blackness canceled it out. It got darker and darker until the only light that could be seen was from the four candles in the circle.

"Bind me!" it screamed.

Wind blasted around the room like a tornado. The force pulled at me, but so far it didn't move me.

It held its hands over its head. The light flickered in the room, jumping back and forth from the complete darkness to the sunlight and back again. The demon's face clenched. The skin stretched over the cheeks so tightly I thought it might tear. It grimaced hard. The teeth broke further and a few fragments fell out of its mouth.

The gusts picked up. I toppled over and the force of the winds pushed me across the floor until I slammed into the barrier of the magic circle. My head swam, my mouth dried, and my skin felt like it was going to be ripped from my body. I don't know why the wind could come into the magic circle, but the demon and I were separated by it.

Then the child became the demon. The skin rippled as if something was underneath it. When the rippling stopped, its skin appeared scaled. It snarled and the breath came out like green steam. The smell that radiated from it was like a cross between curdled milk and charred human flesh. The pupils of its eyes elongated—the eyes of a viper.

I forced myself to stand against the wind, but it was too strong.

"No one will bind me. No one will bind Asmodeus!"

The plaster of the ceiling cracked and bent. The howling of the wind deafened me. It stood up, somehow not bothered by the wind at all. Its hair didn't even move. Its mouth opened as if it was laughing, but I could hear nothing but the wind.

I forced my foot through the salt, breaking the circle. I paused, keeping my footing. The wind forced my feet to scuff along the floor until I slammed against the wall. I searched around for the mirror. Then I saw it being forced across the floor by the brutal gales. I gathered what will I had and thrust my hand out against the force and managed to grab it. "Leave her!"

Asmodeus snarled and began to levitate. "This cunt is mine."

The squalls blew harder until I was pressed into the wall with such force I could barely breathe. I held on to the mirror as best as I could. Something invisible pried my fingers away from it—one by one. And then, the blasts ripped the mirror from my grasp.

The wind stopped. I stepped away from the wall. The demon held the mirror in Lucy's small hands.

My heart pounded fast and hard like a beat machine turned up to the highest speed. A great booming vibrated around the room. Lucy gagged and coughed. Three iron nails fell from her mouth, covered in bloody mucus. It smiled then looked at me. "Shall I gut you, Priest? Dig these little hands in deep?"

I stood there. My feet planted to the floor. I stared it in the bloody eyes. "You won't be gutting me or anyone else."

It laughed, deep and rough. It echoed in my brain and I bent over, the pain of the echo resounding like an explosion. I fought the pain and stood again, forcing myself to push it aside. I held up my hand and made the sign of the cross. "Leave her, you foul being. You denizen of the deep, teller of lies, face of many. You are not welcome here!"

It howled with laughter. "All said to me before. Can't you come up with anything original?"

I wasn't sure how much longer I could take it. It was pulling me toward something dark. The tentacles of such evil reached inside me. "Lead me not into temptation…"

"Oh you'll get more than temptation when I'm done with you. Your sister knows all about that."

I rose up taller. Sweat ran down the back of my neck. I closed my eyes, centering my focus. When I opened my eyes again, something had shifted. My heart calmed. My mind cleared. The world seemed to have stilled.

"Leave her!" The ripples of the force of my scream beat through the air in vivid colors and streams.

It dropped the mirror. The glass shattered across the floor.

"Leave this world for your own. Leave the world of light. Leave this pure child of God!"

"Fucking priests!" it said.

A shard of glass streamed from the frame of the mirror.

I jumped and pressed my back into the wall. I threw my hands over my face, expecting the glass to come flying at me.

The demon would kill me. I knew it.

I heard a loud thump and a bump.

I lowered my hands. Lucy fell to the floor. The shard of glass had been driven through her left eye. Blood spread around her body in a pool. She was dead. The demon had arranged it all.

"Stupid, stupid priest. The girl is ours!" Asmodeus' voice echoed throughout the air.

I howled in rage—my voice sending light, white light around the room. Everywhere my voice reached, the darkness seemed to run from it. Impulsively, I felt my legs travel toward Lucy's body. I made the sign of the cross on her forehead with my finger.

Bang.

The room returned to normal. The darkness had faded.

"It's over, Jimmy," the whispering voice spoke to me. "You've done well."

I glanced around the room. There was no one there. "But she died!"

A hand rested on my shoulder that I could not see.

"Her soul is marked. You marked her. As long as her soul is marked, the Devil cannot do anything with it."

I gazed at my shoulder. Depressions appeared in my shirt where invisible fingers touched me. "But what will happen to Lucy?"

"She'll stay with you until I can reclaim her. I've needed another marker for a long time."

My mouth hung open. "Are you God?"

I heard a soft chuckle. "No, his servant like you. I take care of the gates."

"Peter?" I asked, but then the light in the room dimmed.

I collapsed. My legs no longer wanted to support me. I had lost, but I hadn't failed. It didn't make it any better.

Without thinking, I turned back to Lucy, mentally preparing for the sight of her dead body. My eyelids flicked closed. I needed another second, or two, or three. A soft sound invaded my mind. Some whistling noise like…breathing! I snapped my eyes open. Lucy's chest began rising and falling.

"Will!" I jumped up and ripped open the door. "Goddammit Will, call nine-one-one!"

I hit the alarm button on the recording device outside the door. Then I ran back into the room, took off my shirt, and wrapped it around Lucy's head. I had to slow the bleeding.

I heard a giggle then spun around. A beautiful Lucy stood in the corner. "I'm okay, silly."

I swallowed hard and spied the flashing lights outside the window a few minutes later. Would they believe how it happened at all?

Chapter Thirty-Two

The Sweet Sound of Silence

THE FOOTSTEPS POUNDED up the stairs. Lucy was still breathing, but the other Lucy, the perfect one, stood over in the corner dancing. Every so often she would wave at me.

"Mr. Holiday?" I glanced at the doorway, a uniformed officer stood at the entry. "I'm Sheriff Bedecki."

"Where are the emergency people? She's bleeding too much."

The sheriff nodded. "I had to make sure nothing crazy was going on." He picked up his walkie-talkie and spoke into it. "Bring 'em on up. Scene's safe."

As soon as the EMT's got there, I left Lucy to them. She had a better chance to survive—even if her soul was separated from her body. They put her on a stretcher after they stabilized her as best as they could and took her out of the room.

A tingling sensation burned across my right wrist. When I looked down, an odd tattoo of a cross encircled with seven words in a language I could not read ringed around it. My fingers touched it reverently. "The mark."

After the EMTs disappeared with Lucy, the sheriff stared me in the eyes—hard. "You do that to her?"

"No sir," I said, unflinching, "the demon did."

"Uh huh. How did the 'demon' do it?"

I coughed. "It would be easier if you watched the feed."

"You have video?" He cocked his head to the side. "Okay. Where is it?"

"In the device outside the door."

I led the sheriff to the recording device. Lucy's spirit hovered around, watching everything. I didn't want her to see the scene of her death again, but I had no way of telling her that. It wouldn't be good to have the sheriff see me talking to thin air.

#

After Tor was off to the hospital with Lucy's body, the sheriff took the rest of us to the station for questioning. It was a small station, a nondescript grey block building. The sign was in good condition and the building had been repainted.

It was the first time I'd been questioned by the police. They ushered me into an empty grey room with a long table and a few cheap chairs. A camera rested in the corner of the ceiling not unlike the one we used with Lucy.

I sat waiting for around two hours before the sheriff came in.

Lucy's spirit kept wandering the room, exploring things. Luckily, she didn't try to make me laugh or anything.

"Mr. Holiday," the sheriff said. His bloodshot eyes searched my face.

"Yes, sir."

He sat in one of the chairs near me. "Explain to me how an ex-priest ends up performing an exorcism."

I sighed. "Will asked me. At first, I wasn't even sure she was possessed. When it became clear she was, we contacted Father John."

The sheriff motioned for me to go on.

"The church sanctioned the exorcism, but couldn't get an

exorcist here for six months. In this country, the few exorcists are in high demand. With Lucy's health the way it was, she couldn't wait six months. So Will and Tor asked me to exorcise Lucy."

The sheriff leaned back in his chair. "That video's the damnedest thing I've ever seen. Weird crap over the years at Blackmoor."

I nodded.

"Got an AV guy from the appliance repair shop to look at it. He confirmed it wasn't tampered with." He sighed. "My grandpa was the one who found old Black, you know?"

I stared at him. "No, I didn't know that."

He nodded. "That's a bad house. Should be burned to the ground."

"At this point, the Andersens will probably agree with you."

"Gotta ask you to stick around. Least for a while."

"That's fine. Any motels around here?" I couldn't go back to that house. Not now.

"Got a Day's Inn out on seventy-seven."

"That's where I plan to be."

He reached into his pocket and handed me a card. "Call me when you have the particulars."

"Will do."

Lucy didn't wake up, at least her body didn't. It was comatose in the hospital for an indeterminate amount of time. What I'd come to think of as the real Lucy was with me. Sometimes it was hard not to laugh at her antics. The doctors said she was in a persistent vegetative state. After about a month, Sheriff Bedecki told me I could go home.

Will and Tor paid for my hotel room. Why they did it, I didn't know. It was like they wanted to repay me somehow, but couldn't stand to be around me. I didn't blame them.

They stayed at the hotel too. I don't know what they

planned to do about Blackmoor. I never asked. We kept our conversations light.

When I left, all I got was a simple nod from Will.

#

Four months later…

I was trying to get everything ready for Tabby to move in. We decided we were going to give it another go. At least I'd finally found some freelance graphic design work. I lost my job in the month it took me waiting around to see if I was going to be charged with anything connected to what I'd come to think of as *the incident.*

Lucy was still with me. I hadn't broken that part to Tabby yet. I hoped she wouldn't hold it against me.

I'd finished cleaning the house. Tabby was set to arrive tomorrow with the U-Haul. It was about eight, and I was tired.

"You're going to get a phone call," Lucy said, pushing a magazine in the middle of the coffee table.

"When?"

"Three," she said in a sing-song voice.

Dread licked up my spine. "Not again."

Lucy nodded. "Yup."

"You going to help me?" I asked.

She smiled her bright smile, teeth perfect, eyes dancing. "You bet!"

THE END

Thank you for reading! Find book two in the Marker Chronicles, SORROW'S EDGE, in 2016, and catch the included special excerpt next!

Please sign up for the City Owl Press newsletter for chances to win special subscriber-only contests and giveaways as well as receiving information on upcoming releases and special excerpts.

www.danielledevor.com

@sammyig

All reviews are welcome and appreciated. Please consider leaving one on your favorite social media and book buying sites.

For books in the world of romance and speculative fiction that embody Innovation, Creativity, and Affordability, check out City Owl Press at www.cityowlpress.com.

See the next page for a sneak peek at book two in the
Marker Chronicles,

BOOK TWO OF THE MARKER CHRONICLES
SORROW'S EDGE

BY: DANIELLE DEVOR

Coming Soon from City Owl Press

Chapter One

It's All Coming Back to Me Now

AS LUCY PREDICTED, I got the phone call at three. I was really starting to hate the true "witching hour." I needed sleep, dammit.

I let the phone ring a few times, hoping that whoever was on the other end would hang up. I wasn't that lucky. I rose, grabbed my phone off the nightstand, and swiped the screen.

"Mr. Holiday?" the man asked when I grunted into the receiver.

"You realize it's three a.m., right?" My head hit the pillow. I did not want to be doing this right now.

The man sighed. "It couldn't be helped. We need you."

I twitched. Who the hell was this guy anyway? Kind of presumptuous to call somebody at random this late when you've never met the person on the other end. His mother clearly never taught him manners.

I glanced around the room. The light in the corner was still on. I'd gotten into the habit of sleeping with a light on ever since Sorrow's Point. Yeah, it was irrational, but hey, I was trying to keep the darkness at bay. Lucy was sitting on the floor in front of the TV. I could barely see the program through her. Her hair was as pale as usual—so blonde it looked almost white. She was wearing the same white nightgown she always did.

"How did you get my number?" I had to know. I mean, I doubted Will would suggest me to someone else.

"You came highly recommended."

That was news to me. Only a very small group of people knew I did something besides graphic design. "By who?"

"That's not important right now. You're needed. That's what should matter."

I sat up. Not important to him, maybe, but it sure as hell was important to me. This guy was starting to piss me off. "Listen. I'm not about to traipse around and do whatever the hell it is you want me to do when you won't tell me who you are and you won't tell me who told you about me."

"O'Malley said you'd be difficult."

I froze. Father O'Malley had been the one who allowed me to see the church as a vocation when I was a kid. But there was one problem. He'd been dead since before I left the church. I didn't care where he got the information. That was a low blow. Still, though, he having known about O'Malley at all had me nervous.

"I'm going to hang up now. I'd appreciate it if you didn't call here again."

"No, wait!"

The desperation in his voice was the only thing that kept me from ending our little call. "All right. I'm listening."

"O'Malley told me about you in a dream. When I woke up, your phone number was scrawled on my hand."

Yeah, that was definitely the weird I had experience with. Having a dead person talk to him in a dream wasn't so different from having a disembodied soul speak to me in a nightmare. My life was *really* interesting. Though, I'd never drawn on my body in my sleep. That was a new one. "So who is it that needs an exorcism?"

#

The guy hung up. I swear I heard the phone hit the cradle. *Who uses an old phone like that anymore?* I almost threw my cell against the wall. I mean, what the fuck was that? Wake me up in the middle of the night for what? A stupid prank?

I scratched the sleep out of my eyes and looked over at Lucy. "Don't you ever sleep?"

She smiled at me, her blue eyes sparkling. "I don't have to."

I shook my head. Of course a kid would think it's great to not sleep. I, on the other hand, needed my rest—weird phone calls or not. And if someone else called, I'd probably be looking at a murder charge.

"Do you think Tabby will like me?" Lucy asked. She stayed dressed in her little delicate white nightgown. I wasn't sure if it was her favorite or if there was something else at work keeping her dressed like that. When I'd done her exorcism she sure wasn't in frills.

That was the question, wasn't it? I'd been toying with the idea of not telling Tabby, but it appeared that was no longer an option. And, with my luck, she would eventually see Lucy, freak out, and the whole thing would be blown out of proportion.

"I'm sure she will," I swallowed the words, not sure of their truth, "after she gets used to the idea."

Lucy stared at me for a bit. I could tell she wasn't buying it. I needed to start remembering there was more to her than a regular six-year-old.

"It will all work out," I told her. "Eventually." Part of that was me trying to convince my own conscience. Only so much weird a normal person could take, and I figured I was probably getting close to the threshold.

"Uh huh," Lucy said, then went back to watching the TV. How she could just sit in front of the TV for hours on end, I didn't know. It was like she became somehow hypnotized by it.

I laid my head back down on the pillow. I wished I could go

back to sleep. I wished I could stop worrying about weird phone calls. I wished…who was I kidding? I was screwed. Again.

#

By the time the sun was stabbing into my eyes like a pincushion, I'd gotten maybe four hours of sleep. Leave it to Lucy to put voice to my fears. My best option was to tell Tabby outright, and while I knew she was used to weird things, how could I be sure this wouldn't be so far left field she'd think I was insane? Of course, she probably already thought I was nuts, but that was beside the point.

I got out of bed and crawled into the shower. The heat and the steam felt good. I needed to relax, but it wasn't like my life lent itself to a lot of down time. My shoulders were so tense that they hurt every time I tried to move my head. I ran my hands over my hair, getting the last of the soap out.

I needed a hobby. Something calming, like fishing. Too bad it was still a little too cold for that. And I wasn't the most patient person in the world. Yeah, fishing was out.

"Jimmy?" I heard Lucy ask through the door.

I turned off the shower so I could hear her better. "What?"

"The phone's ringing."

Again? I grabbed a towel off the rack, wrapped it around my waist, and headed toward the door. Out of the corner of my eye, I saw a brown disembodied head pass through the mirror. I didn't even flinch. I left the bathroom and held the towel around my middle. No sense in giving Lucy an eyeful of stuff she didn't need to be exposed to. Yeah, she was a spirit, but she was still alive too, and I wasn't about to take anymore of her innocence away when the demon had taken most of it.

The phone had already stopped ringing. I picked it up anyway. There wasn't a notification of voicemail, so I looked at the missed calls. I was almost afraid that Mr. Creepy had called again. But no, it was Tabby. I called her back and waited. I started to hang up when she answered.

"What the hell are you doing?" she asked.

I was glad she couldn't see me roll my eyes. If she could, I would have been socked in the arm. "Um. Getting a shower?"

She made a grunting noise that sounded like she was trying to move something heavy. I could imagine her pushing her long red hair out of the way while she tried to get a handle on the boxes. I loved her hair.

"Did anything weird happen last night?" she asked.

How did she know? Sometimes her insight was too creepy. "Yeah. There was a phone call."

"Another one?" There was a little hint of sarcasm in her voice. I wasn't sure if she was annoyed with me, the situation, or packing.

"Well, maybe. It's kind of complicated." Well, as complicated as *Attack of the Killer Tomatoes*, but whatever.

"Everything is always complicated with you, Jimmy. When I get there, I'll be expecting details. But is this something you want to do again?"

Good question. Heck, I still wasn't even sure if the phone call had been a stupid prank. "I'm not sure if I have a choice."

"I thought God was all about free will and all that?"

Well, for normal people, he was. I gave some of that away when I became a priest, and despite being de-frocked, some of the stuff I swore to, I still kind of believed in. "To a point, yeah. But we could talk theology for hours."

"True."

"How much longer till you get here?" Having her here was going to be a change, but I viewed it as something good.

She sighed. "Who the fuck knows? I've got so much stuff to pack."

If I hadn't had to get my house moved around for her to put her stuff in here, I would have been up there to help her. "Okay, okay. I'll stop pestering you."

"If I didn't want to be pestered, I wouldn't have called you." She laughed.

I smiled. She liked me bugging her. "I miss you."

"I miss you too," she replied.

Too bad her witchiness wasn't strong enough. Too bad she couldn't wave her hand and have her things pack themselves. But real magic didn't work that way. "I'll let you go. Get back to packing."

"Okay. Be good."

I laughed. "Always." Well, that was a lie. I played being good well, but I was way too ornery to do what I was supposed to and leave it at that.

#

Lucy gaped at the TV. Normally, I wouldn't find this strange, especially with her obsession with the digital airways, but she was watching a horror film.

"What are you doing?" I asked.

She spun to me. "This is so fake."

Some evil creature was ripping out a guy's stomach on the screen. Spirit or not, she was six. I knew her mom and dad wouldn't want her watching stuff like this. I grabbed the remote off the coffee table and turned it off.

"Hey!" she said.

"Hey, nothing. I don't have permission from your parents for you to be watching something like that." I wasn't sure if I had a kid, if I'd want them watching horror at her age either.

She glared at me. "I've seen worse anyway."

Yeah, she had. She was this sweet kid. But I couldn't deny she'd seen and experienced worse. If I could, I'd take it all away.

"I hope you can put that behind you one day."

Her pale hair flew around her head as she shook it. "I'd rather have him where I can see him."

I couldn't argue with that. We'd both seen too much. And knew too much.

Sorrow's Point had been hell. I still had dreams about the demon. Fighting for Lucy's soul had been one of the hardest things I'd ever done. Tabby, well, she'd fought too. It'd been a miracle I'd been able to stop the thing before it attacked Tabby worse than it had. And then, added to it all, I became the guardian of Lucy's soul.

I hoped she could get reunited with her body and forget all this shit. If not, there was no way she was going to have a social life. I didn't even want to think about the possibility of spirit babies.

Great. Now I had something else I needed to forget.

#

The rest of the morning I finished straightening up the house. No sense in letting Tabby freak out about the state of the place. I wasn't the type of guy to live in a pigsty, but I had some clutter. It had to go, for the time being at least. I mean, Tabby needed more than a path to move her things into the house. My books needed to be moved off the floor. After rearranging things, I'd even managed to make space in the living room for her to add some bookcases. Between the both of us, we had a lot of books.

Lucy stayed in front of the TV. Mostly to stay out of the way, I think. I didn't know if items passing through her hurt. She'd never said. Of course, she'd been quiet all day. She hadn't spoken to me since I'd refused to let her watch the horror film.

I was walking into the kitchen when I suddenly noticed all of the light in the house was dimmer, almost as if something was blocking out the sun. I went to the front door, opened it, and looked out. The sky turned clear yet darker somehow. Something big, yet not totally opaque, blocked out part of the sun. I did not want to think about omens, but if I'd paid attention to the signs with Lucy, maybe things would have turned out better.

The sky darkening with no clouds was a hell of a clue, but of what? The dark sky could mean a storm was coming, but there weren't any storm clouds that I could see. Beyond weird.

"Are you seeing this, Lucy?" I knew she could hear me. So far, it didn't seem to matter how far away from her I was, she always heard me. I peered at the sky, probably doing a damn good meerkat impression.

"You need to listen," she said from behind me.

To what? I was looking at stuff, not hearing anything weird. I turned around. "Lucy, the only thing you were talking about was some dumb horror movie."

She nodded. "And you didn't listen."

I closed the door and crouched in front of her. Maybe I should start paying better attention. "What did that movie have to do with this?" I pointed at the sky.

She shrugged. "Doesn't matter now. He's coming." Then she disappeared.

"Who's coming?" I asked, hoping she wouldn't ignore me. She didn't answer. This was so not good.

The doorbell rang.

I would like to say that the doorbell was connected to someone who could help me with all of this, but no dice. It was the postman delivering a package. I probably should have thought about this more, but I was more worried over the dark sky and Lucy than the package.

I opened the door and stared for a minute. I don't know what I was expecting. Maybe some tall guy in black who could take over and save the day. But no, the delivery man shoved this box toward me. I grabbed it, and he left. Nothing weird about the exchange. The box was square, about fourteen by fourteen and six inches tall. It wasn't real heavy. I held it up to my ear. No ticking. Not that I knew of anyone who would send me a bomb, but hey, you couldn't be too careful.

I lowered the box, closed the door, and walked into the living room in a daze. I felt like I hadn't slept for four days. Something had wiped me out.

"What's that?" Lucy asked. The sunlight from the window was passing through her. A shadow shaped on the floor, not quite corporeal.

"I have no idea."

After walking into the kitchen to get some scissors, I leaned against the counter and glared at the package. It was a regular brown shipping box with clear packing tape. No name on the return address—just an address in Tombstone, Arizona. I didn't know anyone in Arizona and, to be honest, getting a package from a place called Tombstone didn't leave me with a fuzzy feeling. I had enough of this omen shit. I didn't need to be hit over the head with a cinder block for God's sake.

I took a deep breath and sliced through the tape on the box with the scissors. Nothing happened. No explosions. Small comfort.

"Is that a good idea?" Lucy asked. She was standing in the doorway to the kitchen now. It was kind of disconcerting to have a kid around that you could never hear walk around the house. I was always thinking she was up to something just because she was quiet.

I shrugged. "We won't know unless I open it."

"That's what that girl thought when she opened that box in that movie."

I set the scissors down on the counter. "Just what have you

been watching when I go to sleep at night?" I vaguely remembered seeing a trailer for a movie like that. Something about a possession. She didn't need to watch that type of stuff. *How in the hell do you get a therapist for a spirit?*

"Stuff."

I rolled my eyes. *Yeah, stuff. Great.* That left me feeling relaxed about the whole thing. *Right.*

I opened the flaps on the box and took a deep breath. Inside was something taped in bubble wrap. I picked up the scissors again and cut through the tape like opening the wrappings on a mummy. Nestled amongst the plastic wrap laid a silver flask with the initials J.H.H. etched into the side of it. I looked back through the packing, but there was no note, no nothing. *Okay, why did someone send me this?*

"Is it okay?" Lucy asked.

"I guess so. No weird smells or anything." Just a silver flask. Nothing weird I could detect about it, only that it was sent to me, but that was beside the point.

She crept over to look at it. I held it down to her level. After a minute, she shrugged and sauntered out of the room.

"Okay. Guess it isn't dangerous," I said to no one.

The lack of danger still had me nervous. Who had sent it, and more importantly, why? I had a sinking suspicion that phone call wasn't a prank after all.

ACKNOWLEDGEMENTS

I'd like to thank my parents for their ability to put up with my horror film obsession and my interest in the unusual. Without their open-mindedness, I wouldn't be the writer I am today.

And then there's Tabby Barber and Julia Long, my hometown crew. Can't thank you guys enough for keeping me straight. And, I can't forget Maer Wilson, your support through the various incarnations of this book has been invaluable.

For the amazing Tina Moss and City Owl Press, I can't put into words how much I appreciate everything you've done for Sorrow's Point. Thanks to her, this book is so much more amazing than it was before.

And, lastly, thanks to my fans for following the journey. I love you all and your support.

ABOUT THE AUTHOR

Named one of the Examiner's 2014 Women in Horror: 93 Horror Authors You Need to Read Right Now, Danielle DeVor has been spinning the spider webs, or rather, the keyboard for more frights and oddities. She spent her early years fantasizing about vampires and watching "Salem's Lot" far too many times. When not writing and reading about weird things, you will find her hanging out at the nearest coffee shop, enjoying a mocha frappuccino.

www.danielledevor.com

ABOUT THE PUBLISHER

City Owl Press is a cutting edge indie publishing company, bringing the world of romance and speculative fiction to discerning readers.

www.cityowlpress.com

Lightning Source UK Ltd.
Milton Keynes UK
UKHW011831060322
399646UK00004B/34